Metaphorosis

May 2018

Beautifully made speculative fiction

Also from Metaphorosis Books

Reading 5X5: Readers' Edition
Reading 5X5: Writers' Edition

Best Vegan Science Fiction & Fantasy

Best Vegan SFF of 2017
Best Vegan SFF of 2016

Metaphorosis Magazine

Metaphorosis: Best of 2017
Metaphorosis: Best of 2016
Metaphorosis 2017: The Complete stories
Metaphorosis 2016: Nearly Complete Stories
Monthly issues

by B. Morris Allen

Susurrus
Allenthology: Volume I
Tocsin: and other stories
Start with Stones: collected stories
Metaphorosis: a collection of stories

Metaphorosis

May 2018

edited by
B. Morris Allen

Metaphorosis Books

Neskowin

ISSN: 2573-136X (online)
ISBN: 978-1-64076-108-7 (e-book)
ISBN: 978-1-64076-109-4 (paperback)

May 2018

Calm Folk, Come Forth!

Adan Berkowitz

The bear stood on its hind legs and roared. Its fur was matted and tangled, brown with hints of orange, and one of its ears was mostly gone. Gray eyes and long sharp teeth. Rancid breath wafted over me, and I pinched my nose. I was pretty sure it was a grizzly. Dad said grizzlies were big, and mean. He said if you got between a grizzly sow and her cubs, you'd better watch out. No baby bears in sight, but I figured there were probably a few tucked away in a nearby den.

"Sorry," I said. "Didn't mean to bother you."

Momma bear didn't accept my apology. She roared again, then clamped her jaws around my head, like a nasty hat that didn't fit. Gooey saliva dripped onto my face, and I frowned. Now I was going to smell like bear drool the rest of the day.

"Leave me alone," I said, annoyed. "I don't have time for this."

As if she'd understood, the bear let go. She gave me a strange look—at least, as strange as a bear could muster—then turned and ran into the trees. My head began to come back together where the grizzly's teeth had split it, and I sighed. If I kept getting sidetracked, this trip was going to take a lifetime.

Sluggishly, I lurched onward while my head fixed itself. I plucked some berries into my mouth to help speed things along, wincing at their tartness.

When I found Mom in Fija Nostra, I would tell her all about the bear, how sharp its teeth had been and how its breath had stunk. We would talk about the places we'd been and the things we'd seen, and then we'd go home and she would be herself again. That's what I wanted to believe, but in all honesty, I wasn't sure.

The sun drifted down into its hiding place, reminding me of Mom's dark moods her last few months on the mountain, how she'd become almost like a different person. Dad assured me we'd get through it, though I could tell he was worried. 'Out of darkness comes light' was one his sayings, and he really believed it.

As if to prove this was true, a spark of flame flickered in the murky distance. Figuring it might belong to someone who could point me toward Fija Nostra, I headed that way. Soon I came upon a campsite, two men beside a small tent. One of the men chopped wood on a tree stump while the other ate onions from a sack next to the fire. The man stopped chopping and looked at me. Like the grizzly, he had dark brown hair, though not as matted. The other man took a loud bite of his onion. This one had silvery blond hair like Mom. Both wore black flowing robes that seemed to swallow them up.

"Who the hell're you?"

"Hi," I said. "I'm looking for my Mom."

"Do I look like your goddamned mom, guy?"

"Relax, Prowie," said the blond man near the fire. "What's your name, son?"

"Ben," I offered.

"Bennie. Come here, Bennie boy. I'm going to cut you up and eat you for lunch." Prowie raised the ax over his head. Then he put it back down, laughing. "Just what I thought. Look at him, Kaz. Not even a flinch. You're not afraid one bit, are you Ben?"

I stared at him blankly.

"Of course you aren't. You're a Lazzie for sure."

"Now Prowie, you don't know that. He might just be a little off in the head."

"I saw a grizzly," I said proudly. "I'd lay odds on it." I wasn't certain what that meant, but Mom always used to say it when she was sure of something.

The two men looked at each other, then burst out laughing. I laughed too.

"Where you from, son?" Kaz asked. "You can't be more than twelve years old."

"Up on the mountain," I replied, "and I'm twelve-and-a-half, thank you."

"Are you a Lazzie?"

"I've never heard that word before."

"It means you don't get scared, because you've nothing to fear. You don't feel pain."

"No," I said. "My Dad says pain is useless, since we just come back together anyway."

"Is that so?"

Prowie smiled at me. His teeth were yellow and brown, and they slanted in different directions. "Want to give me some help, Bennie lad? You can steady the wood. Just grab the chunk and hold it for me."

Prowie scooped up a piece of firewood and balanced it on the stump. "Just like that, see?"

I nodded. Prowie's hand drifted away and I held the wood firmly, making sure not to let it wobble.

Kaz rose, frowning. "That's enough, Prowie."

Prowie turned to me, still smiling. "All right. Keep her straight now, Bennie." He raised the ax above his head. "Ready?" I nodded.

"One....two..."

Prowie brought the ax down with a mighty *whack*. The blade missed the wood and instead split my wrist. My right hand dropped sadly to the ground, and blood came out of the stump where it had been. Kaz gasped. Prowie looked at me with wide eyes.

"Sorry," I said. "I must have flinched."

Prowie continued to stare, mouth hanging open. He tossed the ax away.

"See," he said, weakly. "I told you."

"I think I'm going to be sick," Kaz said.

"Doesn't hurt?"

"Nope," I said. I pointed at the sack of onions. "Mind if I grab one?"

Whenever something like this happened, I'd be sluggish for a while if I didn't eat. Dad said it had something to do with the conservation of energy, but I never really paid much attention. Honestly, that stuff was kind of boring.

"Look," Kaz said. His face very white among the flames. "It's already starting to grow back."

They were pointing at my right arm. A little nub had formed there. I steadied the wood with my left hand and turned back to Prowie.

"Should we try again?" I asked.

"We can't spend the night with him here," Kas said. He and Prowie sat close to each other, their black cloaks rippling in the night breeze. They were whispering, but I could still hear them. "He's giving me the heebies."

"You was just telling me to leave him alone."

"That was before I saw the trick with his hand."

I watched them, unsure. The fire was almost out.

"I saw one of them once," Kaz said. His voice was unsteady. "Lanky guy, like an acrobat. A showman. He would climb to the top of the tallest flagpole in town and jump off headfirst. He'd go *splat* on the ground, just like that," Kaz clapped his hands together, "and then a few minutes later he'd be back up doing it again. People tossed him coins."

Prowie shrugged.

"Ah, this one's harmless. A babe lost in the woods. Hell, maybe he can guard our gear while we doze. You don't hafta sleep, do you Bennie?"

I frowned. Prowie was wrong. I didn't get tired that often, but when I did, I slept and dreamed, same as anybody.

"Are you nuts?" Kaz said. He kept running his hands through his silvery hair. "I'm not sleeping with him watching us."

"You're a 'gina, you know that?"

"He shouldn't be here," Kaz said. There was a new coldness in his voice. "He should be under the sea. Under the rocks where his kind belong."

"I'm happy to be moving on," I said. "I didn't mean any trouble."

"There's a Nav Servo east of here," Prowie said. It might be able to sort you out."

"How will I know where to find it?"

"It looks just like a big compass. You can't miss it."

I smiled. "Okay. Thanks."

"Don't meddle with it," Prowie called after me. "It's got security."

"You moron, he's a Lazzie, what's it to him?"

As I walked on, their arguing voices drifted away. The night insects were out, composing their symphony of clicks, chirps, and drones. Sometimes it even sounded a little like the music Mom and Dad used to play back home. A sharp pang of homesickness struck me. But I wasn't going to quit. Not until I found Mom and brought her back to the mountain. Besides, now I was curious to know what a Lazzie was.

Not long after, I came upon the Nav Servo. It was a big compass, just like

Prowie said. Round, made of some shiny, brassy material. Its face was topped with thick glass, and there was a single dark needle slowly spinning clockwise. Behind it was a large broken tube, its sides a swampy green color.

The glass felt smooth and cool. A voice spoke: "Warning: tampering with me risks death by electric shock. I contain ionizing radiation. Do not attempt to vandalize or deface me. Repairs should only be performed by a licensed professional."

The voice was calm but firm. I couldn't tell if it was a man or a woman. I said, "Hello!"

"Hello," said the Nav Servo. "I am Sutton, the Navigation Servomechanism for the Northern Autonomous region of Greater Suttony."

"I'm Ben. Nice to meet you Sutton. How are you?"

"I am well. And yourself?"

"Not bad," I said. "Sutton, what's a Lazzie?"

The needle spun wildly beneath the glass.

"I'm sorry. Apart from basic pleasantries, I am only allowed to answer questions pertaining to navigation. This is required by law to limit my superfluous knowledge and prevent sentience."

"I see." I scratched my cheek. "Well, I'm on my way to Fija Nostra. Can you tell me how to get there?"

"Of course!" Pleasure in Sutton's voice. "You are the second person to ask directions to this location in the past two days. By tube, the estimated travel time to Fija Nostra is .34 seconds. By air, the estimated travel time is nine hours, 20 minutes. By heavy rail, the estimated time is 12 hours 11 minutes, allowing for transfer. By foot, the estimated time is upward of 30 days."

"Sounds like the tube is fastest."

"Yes. Unfortunately, the tube network is currently out of service. I apologize for any inconvenience."

I looked over at the greenish tube, cracked everywhere. No surprise it was broken. Sutton's needle whirled around like a happy dog's tail.

"The latitude and longitude of Fija Nostra is as follows..." Sutton recited a long string of numbers. They sounded familiar, but I couldn't remember where I'd heard them, and I didn't understand what they meant.

"That doesn't help," I said. "Which direction do I go?"

Sutton's needle swung around to the southeast, where it locked firmly in place.

"Unfortunately, my knowledge of transportation options is limited to the Greater Autonomous Region of Suttony. However, there is a bicycle in the direction you are headed which may be useful. There is a high probability it has been abandoned by its previous owner, as it has been unused for 3 months. The bicycle needs maintenance, but should be functional. I apologize that this is my only suggestion, but it will be faster than traveling on foot."

"A bike!" I said. "That's great!"

The needle spun merrily around, locking back in the southeast position. The path to Fija Nostra. I thanked Sutton.

"My pleasure, Ben. Safe travels on your journey."

Walking through the overgrown forest, I nearly blundered right by a metal rack covered in leaves and vines. Leaning there, almost completely camouflaged by the foliage, was a yellow bicycle. Its tires were flat, and the chain was rusted, but luckily there was a small pack slung around the seat with some air cartridges, patches, and rubbing alcohol. I figured it all belonged to a tube traveler who'd forgotten to return. Or maybe the system had broken before they could. Either way, it didn't seem like they were coming back, so I didn't feel too bad about taking their stuff.

Dragging the bike from the shrubbery, I wiped down the chain with alcohol until the rust was gone. Then I patched the tires and filled them with air. When I was done, it looked almost new.

"Not a bad job, for a Lazzie," I said. For some reason this made me laugh. I hopped on and pumped the pedals and away I went.

After riding for a few hours, I emerged from the forest onto a large plain, with big brown stalks swaying everywhere. They rustled my face as I passed, a gentle, fuzzy feeling. The plain had a slight downward slope, and I coasted along, barely having to pedal.

I thought of Mom, and how we used to ride bikes together on the mountain. That was before she started to go crazy. Before she heard voices that weren't there and thought the raccoons that foraged through our trashcans were plotting against her. Dad told me that when you've been alive for so long, sometimes the mind starts to break down. He tried to help her with medicines and therapies, even electroshocks, but nothing seemed to work. By the time she ran off, she wasn't the same person I grew up with.

Lost in my daydream, I didn't see the cliff until it was too late. I squeezed the brakes with all my might, but it was no use. I tumbled over the edge. Below, the tops of trees looked like little smudges of green paint. They grew bigger and bigger, and then I hit the rocks and came apart.

When I came back together, there were people standing around me. A group of them, men and women and boys and girls. The only one to approach me was a girl with bright red hair. Smiling, she knelt and put a wet rag against my forehead. I tried to move my arms and legs and couldn't. There were iron shackles around them. The girl with the red hair studied me. She had green eyes, and looked to be around my age.

"Are you okay?" she asked.

"Daphne!" One of the men called out, angrily. "Get away from him!"

The girl named Daphne turned to the man, who was holding a large wooden club.

"Relax," she said, still dotting my forehead with the damp rag. "Does he look like he's going to hurt anyone?"

Another man, with an orange beard hanging to his belly, strode forward and slung Daphne up over his back. She cried out, attacking him with her fists, but she was too small. The man carried her a few paces away and set her down among the rest of the crowd. She did not seem pleased.

The man who had yelled at Daphne stepped forward. He must have been her Dad. He was big, his forehead shiny with sweat.

"We know you're a Lazzie," he said, smacking the club against his open palm with a *thwack*. "Don't try and deny it."

"What does that mean?" I asked, exasperated.

"Don't play dumb with me. Daphne here saw you fall off the cliff. Saw you smash open like an overripe tomato and regrow your parts like a goddamned starfish."

Daphne again pushed her way to the front of the pack. Her hair was frizzy and tangled.

"Leave him alone!" she said. "He wasn't bothering anyone. He was dead and then he came back to life. It's a miracle, is what it is."

"Daphne love, it's no miracle," said the man. "It's a menace. I've heard about towns ravaged by these creatures. Not the women…"

He turned back to me, waving the club in my face. "No, your kind isn't usually interested in procreation. Instead you get bored. First you tear apart the livestock, to see what it's like. Then you move on to the people."

"My name's Ben," I said. There was a prickly feeling in my chest. "Ben Wells. I haven't torn anyone apart. I'm just looking for my Mom. If you don't want me here, I'll keep going."

"We should listen to him," said one of the women. "If he wants to move on, maybe he won't bother us."

"Maybe?" The man with the club snorted. "You want to risk the children's lives on maybe? Sure, maybe he'll keep on. Or maybe he'll track back around and slaughter us as we sleep. We're lucky we've got this one in chains already. I say we wall him off deep in a cave and let him rot."

"No!" Daphne yelled. "That's wicked! He's just a boy. He didn't do anything wrong!"

"It isn't up for debate," said the man with the club. He motioned at the others.

Some approached eagerly, while others hesitated. In the end, they all came forward. The men lifted me up and the sky tilted like a pendulum. I shouted in protest, but they were too strong. They marched me through the woods, into a yawning cave. It was pitch dark inside, everything furry with moss and mildew. Skittering insects darted over my feet. The man with the club looked at me, his mouth squirming strangely, like an earthworm after rain. Then he turned away.

They left me there, propped against the cave wall. The light from the entrance was slowly blotted out, bit by bit, like an eclipse. Soon it was so dark I couldn't see anything, not even my feet in the irons below me.

After a while it was nighttime—I could only tell because of the bats, their leather wings flapping against my face. It tickled, but I couldn't scratch. I wasn't used to such total darkness. It felt like a storm cloud, smothering me, and there was a peculiar sensation in my stomach. The only way I could describe it was when I read a story a long time ago, about a big boat that crashed into an iceberg and sank beneath the water. My stomach was that boat. It was a new feeling, but not a good one.

To keep my mind off the dark, I tried to imagine home. But instead of happy times, my thoughts kept returning to when Mom left the mountain. I had been so busy hunting for bugs that I didn't even realize she was gone. But by nightfall she hadn't come back. And Dad's face told me she wasn't going to. It was unthinkable. She hadn't even said goodbye.

I'd found a flier in Mom's things after she left. I could see it now in my mind, almost like it was shimmering in the darkness. It said:

Calm Folk, Come Forth!

You are old.

You are tired.

You are ready to ascend.

It's time for a well-deserved rest. Come to beautiful Fija Nostra, and take the next step with us.

Latitude: 3° 36′ 32″ S
Longitude: 144° 35′ 18″ E

Note: We at Fija Nostra charge a nominal fee.

Please contact us for more details.

Dad wouldn't tell me what it meant, but one thing was obvious—Mom was headed to this place called Fija Nostra. I told Dad I was going there to bring her home, and he forbade it. He said I was too young for such a trip, and that finding her was his job. But I was fed up with waiting around.

A scraping sound jolted me back to reality. Suddenly from nothing I saw a flicker of light, growing brighter and brighter, and then there were three men standing at the mouth of the cave, with Daphne leading them.

Daphne watched with arms crossed as one of the men unlocked my irons.

"Kept picturing my own boy in here," he said, as my shackles fell away. "Don't make a fool of me, son."

I assured him I wouldn't. Leaping down to the cave floor, I smiled at Daphne. Her hair was very red, and her eyes were very green.

"You're lucky I like you," she said, smiling back at me.

"Hurry now," said one of the men. "Don't come back here."

"You have to go," Daphne said. "Run. Head straight and turn left at the sawmill. Don't stop until you reach the water."

She leaned in and kissed my cheek. Another new sensation came over me, but unlike the sinking ship, this one was lovely. It was like I had swallowed one of the nearby bats and it was fluttering around in my stomach. I wanted to stay, but I knew I couldn't, so I ran, taking only one look back and seeing the men rolling the heavy rock in front of the cave entrance.

I ran through forests and swamps and thorn bushes and peach groves, all sorts of smells flowering around me, blackberries and skunk and sweet berries and jasmine and pine. I ran until I saw the sawmill, its cracked wooden wheel reminding me of the flat bicycle tires. I ran until Daphne and her village were nothing but a memory. I ran until I reached a tall cliff overlooking the ocean, the air tangy with salt and sand, the sun an orange flame, the sea a frothing churn below. The way forward was uncertain, but I knew I had to keep moving. Taking one last moment to savor the view, I spread my arms and dove into the water.

When I came back together, I was on the ocean floor. My feet sank into mud, silt swirling around me. Bubbles drifted up from my nose. I kicked my feet and began to swim, just like I used to in the lake back home. I swam for a long time. At times sunlight pierced the gloom, revealing the undersea world. Great undersea caverns, endless watery gorges, sea life of every size and shape. Neon fish, shiny fish, fish with long tentacles and fish with lanterns inside them, starfish and angler fish and colorful sea anemones shivering against one another. Every so often I rose back to the surface for a few gulps of air, letting daylight shine through me. Sometimes I slept, floating on my back beneath a sky embroidered with stars, alone but for the gentle bob of the waves and the milky glow of the moon. I swam among sharks and whales, groups of dolphins racing to and fro, creatures I'd only read about. I swam for so long I thought I might be swimming forever. But eventually the ocean floor began to slope, up and up, until I emerged onto a beach.

Shaking water from my hair, I found an island paradise. Sand, waves, palm trees, coconuts, birds flying in circles above, and a leafy jungle opposite the sea. I walked for a while along the beach, eventually coming upon a boat that had been tied to a small wooden dock built in a calm lagoon.

There was a woman near the boat, using a long stick to scrape strange growths off its underside. Another woman walked along the beach, carrying a load of wood in her arms and bobbing her head from side to side to see where she was going. When she spotted me she froze, and the wood went tumbling onto the ground. I jogged over and gathered them. The woman had light hair tied back, and dark brown eyes. Her skin was smooth and white, without a crease on it, and there was a tiredness about her that made me think of Mom.

"Who are you?" the woman asked. I told her my name was Ben, and I'd just come from the sea.

"My word," she said. "You're but a child. I didn't know there were any of you left."

The second woman joined us. She was tall and thin, stork-like, with dark hair and loose clothing that flapped in the breeze.

"Are you two Lazzies?" I asked them earnestly. The women looked at each other and burst out laughing.

"Yes, we've been called that," said the woman with light hair. "I'm Ruth, and this is Ali."

"Everyone's been calling me that, too."

"If you were swimming across the ocean, I'd say it's a safe bet."

"Would you lay odds on it?"

They laughed again.

"I'm headed to Fija Nostra," I said. "I'm looking for my Mom there."

They looked at each other.

"Your mother is there, you say?"

"I'm sure of it."

Ali nodded slowly.

"Everyone who ends up in this godforsaken part of the world is going to Fija Nostra. What do you say Ruth, should we give him a ride?"

"He doesn't have any—" Ruth stopped. Ali shook her head back and forth very slightly, like Ruth had said something wrong.

"That's not our problem."

"I'd like to hear more about his parents. Had to take some work to make him."

"We could use an extra hand for the rigging. Do you know how to tie knots, Ben?"

I nodded. We left later that day, Ali pulling up the anchor and using her big stick to push the boat away from the beach. Ruth steered while Ali navigated. I asked how long the journey would be, and they told me we'd be sailing for at least a week.

There was plenty of work to do on board. I helped raise ropes and tie knots, even though I made them sloppy at first and they showed me how to do it better. One morning, Ali was cooking breakfast and asked me to fetch her some potatoes from the hold. I followed the cramped passage down to the belly of the ship. It led to a small chamber filled with cans and burlap sacks. Opening the sack I thought held the potatoes, I instead caught a flash of something shiny. It was full of gold bars. Puzzled, I stared for a moment before closing it again. I found the real potatoes and brought them up, then asked Ali what the gold was for. She told me not to worry about it, but I wondered.

After a few more days of sailing, Ruth said we were nearing Fija Nostra. I smelled the smoke before I saw it—sour, like rotten eggs. Then it appeared, rising from the island in plumes. As gray as the eyes of the grizzly had been. The smoke came from a rock formation that stretched across the entire island, low and flat, like a dinner plate. I asked Ruth if it was a volcano, and she nodded. Ali anchored the ship and we bobbed in the port, waiting. I imagined everything I would say to Mom once I found her.

At first, Fija Nostra looked like heaven. Lush tropical trees, lagoons and waterfalls, and straw huts dotted the shoreline. But there was also an unsettling quiet in the air. Only the cawing seabirds above made much noise. The smoke turned everything dark and overcast, throwing shadows across the island.

Before we even made it off the boat, a voice yelled: "Stop right there!"

A group of men waited at the edge of the pier. They wore crisp white shirts and brown pants, their skin tanned from the sun. All of them were quite large, and some carried long spears.

"Lazzies?" one of the men asked. Ali shouted back an affirmative.

"You have the fee?"

Ali pulled a gold bar from her cloak. She tossed it down and one of the men caught it.

"Plenty more in the hold."

The man rubbed his hands over its smooth surface and nodded.

There was a terrific clanking noise, and a mechanical gangway extended from the dock. I started to follow it down to the shore, but one of the men blocked my way.

"Hold on. What's a kid doing here?"

"He hitched a ride with us," Ruth said nervously.

"You paying for him too?"

There was a silence.

"He's not—he's looking for his mother."

"His mother?" The man turned around and had a short discussion with the others.

"Fine. You two come through. We'll bring the boy into administration. Find out what his deal is. If he causes any trouble, send him to the brig."

I didn't know what a brig was, but the snarling way he said it made me think it couldn't be good. Ali and Ruth waved goodbye to me as they passed, a strange sadness in their eyes, like they knew it was the last we'd see of each other.

One of the men led me off the docks, along a rising path overlooking the island. He wasn't very friendly, prodding me along and cursing under his breath, but I was eager to see Mom, so I did what he said. Below, waves crashed into white foam. The higher we climbed, the better the view. My stomach buzzed with excitement, knowing Mom was nearby. Soon, we were beside the volcano. I smelled the rotten eggs, heard the hiss of steam, saw the gooey lava pooling in crevices. The volcano funneled up to a hole that belched thick gray smoke. Embers shot into the air and fell in slender glowing trails, like spider legs.

Ahead, a boxy building rested on a flat plateau where the ridge leveled out.

Inside was a woman behind a desk, the same white shirt and dark skin as the rest. The man pointed at a bench.

"Sit," he said. "Wait."

I sat. The place was dreary. Yellow paint flaked off the walls and everything smelled stale and musty, like it hadn't been cleaned in a while. The woman behind the desk kept glancing over at me, but she didn't say anything. Other people in white shirts came in and out, and I could hear them whispering. I felt like a circus animal. Finally, I'd had enough. I'd never been very angry back on the mountain, but out in the world it seemed to happen a lot. I stormed over to the desk.

"I need your help," I said. "I need to find my Mom."

She paused. "I'm supposed to wait for word from my boss."

"I don't have time to wait!"

"Okay, okay!" She looked around nervously, like she was afraid of me. "I'll go through the records. See if your mom's been through here."

I followed her into another room. It was full of shelves crammed with thick books and binders, pages spilling out every which way.

"I never seen a kid Lazzie before," she said. "I didn't even know there were any of you around."

"I'm different."

"Yeah, that's for sure. What's your mom's name, son?"

"Ruby. Ruby Wells."

"Wells. All right, give me a second." She pulled some books from the shelves and flipped through them. I waited with my arms crossed. The woman ran her finger over the pages, then stopped. She made a weird sound.

"What is it?"

"Is this her?"

The woman turned the book to me. There she was! A picture of Mom. Curly red hair and tired eyes, but a beaming smile. I couldn't remember the last time I'd seen her smile like that back on the mountain. Beside her was a picture of Dad, his hair longer than I'd ever seen. I was overjoyed.

"Yes! That's her. Where is she?"

"I'm sorry, kid. She got here a few months ago. She already...ascended."

"Huh?"

The lady looked at me like I was dumb.

"You know. She went into the volcano. That's why Lazzies come here. Something about the chemicals in the lava. It's the only way."

"What are you saying?"

"Your mom is dead. She's not coming back."

A sinking feeling. Like when I'd been in the cave, with bats fluttering around me.

"No," I said. "She can't be dead. You must have made a mistake."

"I thought everyone here knew…"

"No," I said again. Everything suddenly went cold. Without another word, I turned and ran out of the building. Ahead, smoke belched up from the rocky funnel toward the overcast sky. If Mom had gone into the volcano, I would find her.

I raced along the ridge, ignoring a crowd of white shirts who had come out to watch me. The next thing I knew, I was at the mouth of the volcano, enveloped in smoke. Below, lava bubbled like stew in a pot. Mom had to be down there somewhere.

I jumped in.

The lava splashed up around me, rising to my knees. I struggled against it, like wading through steaming molasses. Fumes stung my eyes. Beyond was a gaping chasm, leading deeper into the volcano.

"Mom!" I yelled. "Where are you? Mom!"

Something was wrong with my legs, a bad feeling, like they were being etched away. My body sank lower into the lava, and I cried out. Someone called my name. The voice was familiar, but I couldn't place it. My thoughts were jumbled and scattered, consumed by this horrible new sensation. Then a pair of hands lifted me up, out of the lava, carrying me away. I tried to fight, but all my strength had gone. Whoever was holding me was almost completely submerged, only the top of their head visible.

Tossed from the pit, I sprawled onto a hunk of glassy rock. The air felt unexpectedly cool, and I realized with a shock that the lava had burned my clothes off. As I covered myself in embarrassment, my rescuer stagger forward. I must have been seeing things, because the person who rose steaming and sizzling from the lava looked a lot like Dad. The man sank to his knees, gasping for air, and suddenly I knew this was no mirage. It *was* Dad. I never thought he'd leave the mountain, but I'd been wrong. He'd come to save Mom, just like me. My heart swelled with pride. I crawled toward him, but everything began to feel hazy, like a shade being drawn—

I came back together—or at least that's what it felt like—in an underground cavern. The ceiling was so low that the attendant keeping watch could barely stand up straight. I was in a bed, wearing a gown made from palm fronds. A few beds over was Dad, covered in gauze and bandages. His face was charred, and his curly hair had been singed off. I felt awful. He looked like a monster, and it was my fault.

My legs still felt a little weird, but they worked. I went to Dad and he took my hand, smiling.

"That was a silly thing to do," he said. "Too much of your Mom in you."

"How did you—"

"I told you. Finding Ruby was my job. I was too late to save her. So I waited for you. The natives weren't happy, but they let me stay, as long as I cleaned up for them. When word spread that a boy had jumped into the volcano, I knew."

"Why?" My eyes were wet. "Why did Mom leave? Why did she go into the volcano?"

"Don't blame your Mother. She wasn't in her right mind. She's at peace now. It's better this way."

"She didn't even say goodbye."

"She loved you, Ben. You have to be strong."

"I can't."

"You can. You've always been that way. Like Mom."

I sniffed. Dad squeezed my hand tighter.

"I'm fading, Ben. I can feel myself fading. I'm not afraid. I've lived many lives...and I got to have you. You'll live many lives too."

"Dad..."

"Calm children are rarely born. And yet here you are. Here you are."

Dad was mumbling, his words hard to make out. I tried to say more, but his eyes went funny and he stopped answering me. The lava had only come up to my knees, but Dad had been under it completely. The heat was too much, even for him. I waited at his side, I don't know how long. By nightfall, Dad was gone. His body seemed to gleam, melding with the air before coming apart, until all that was left was a fine powder. A scent like honeysuckle in the valley.

I stood up, wiping my eyes. For the first time I noticed my legs were covered in rough, reddish markings that didn't look like they were going away anytime soon.

"What are these?" I asked the attendant, who was pretending to be busy sweeping the floor.

The attendant looked down.

"One hell of a story," he said. I couldn't argue with that.

I emerged from the cavern to calm night breezes. Smells of fish, of sand, of salt. Ahead was the beach, dark and desolate.

How to describe what I felt? Sadness, and a strange sense of freedom. Mom and Dad were gone. But I was still here.

I thought of Daphne, her smile and green eyes, and my heart beat a little quicker. Maybe I would pay her a visit sometime. There was no rush. The world was very big, and there was much to see.

I walked toward the ocean until the water was lapping at my feet. I kept going.

About the story

The story originally began as an old idea I had kicking around about "The Lazarus People," which was about the rise of a technologically advanced people who augmented themselves to live forever. I couldn't think of anything especially interesting to do with the concept, so I stuck it away in the back of my mind. Later, I had a similar idea wondering how a child without any natural instinct for fear might see the world, what kind of journey he might set off on. I only really had the opening scene in mind, where the boy is attacked by a bear and treats it as a minor nuisance. Instead of being wise and weary, I thought a young boy would be an interesting reversal, sort of a play on the "jaded immortal" trope. I remembered the Lazarus People and decided to combine the two ideas into one story.

Ben, the protagonist, is functionally immortal, but he's also a child—maybe the last of his kind—and he's still naïve and immature in many ways. He's never left the mountain where he's grown up, and despite his invulnerability he realizes the outside world can be confusing and illogical, even cruel. In this way, it's a story about a loss of innocence we all go through, presented through a fantastic lens.

I think Ben's upbeat attitude helps lighten what is actually a fairly dark story about fear, suicide, and the dissolution of a family. The Calm Folk, or "Lazzies" in the story are generally taciturn, but its hinted that some of them have become warped and violent, and there's a suggestion that Ben might stray down this path if he's not careful.

The first half of the story came out more as less as I'd imagined it; the second half was more difficult to write, and veered off into some unexpected directions, but I'm happy with where it ended up. It has the feel of a dark fable or fairy tale, which is fairly different from the kind of thing I usually write, and I was pleased to stretch out a bit from my comfort zone.

A question for the author

Q: What is your writing schedule?

A: It depends. For a longer work like a novel, I'll write every day for at least two hours, otherwise it just never gets done. With short stories, I'm much less disciplined. I'll get an idea and write in bursts, with no set schedule. This leads to a lot of unfinished stories, sadly.

About the author

Adan Berkowitz is a writer, musician, and sometime poker player from central New Jersey. In his spare time, he enjoys reading, playing ping-pong, and spending entirely too much time on twitter. If you'd like to reach him there, check out @AdanRaymond.

On the Scales of Dragons

Kathryn Yelinek

High above the island of Dreden, the wind roared in Tala's ears, chilling her despite the warm bulk beneath her, and she wished humans could mindspeak as dragons did. Instead, she rapped her knuckles against one of Kendriley's incised neck scales and spoke *magné,* a minor Word of power that amplified her voice.

"I don't think the people of Dreden want visitors. Any chance those Xs are bones?"

Kendriley dipped her green head to survey the large, dark Xs laid out in intervals along the shore. To warn ships away, Tala guessed, since she doubted anyone had prepared for arrival by dragon.

"Stone, I think," Kendriley said, with a glance back. She might be older and larger than most dragons, but her sleek, feline grace still thrilled Tala after fifteen years of working together. "Probably granite from the cliffs. I'll make a note later."

Tala rapped a scale in acknowledgement. *Everything is worth knowing,* the Library's motto insisted, and as a librarian she knew that any knowledge—be it landmarks or types of stone—could be important.

"Any word from our colleagues?" she called.

"No," Kendriley growled. Tala felt the rumble as much as heard it. "If they are speaking, I cannot hear them."

How can two pairs of librarians simply vanish? Tala shivered and hugged Kendriley closer, relishing her warmth and smoky smell.

Unfriendly Xs aside, Dreden looked similar to many of the other remote islands she and Kendriley visited to collect knowledge. It would take perhaps a day to walk from end to end. In the north, the forest opened onto farm fields too sodden from ongoing spring rains for planting. In the center of the fields huddled the single village. There, Tala hoped, they would discover what had happened to their colleagues from the King's Library.

As they approached, the village women and children fled inside while the men froze, pointing skyward, a typical rural response. By the time Kendriley descended into the village square, the men had gathered in a huddle to watch. They were a ragtag group, from youths to elders, wearing faded coats and patched woolen trousers against the spring rain.

At least they didn't all run away in fear, Tala noted, holding tight as Kendriley folded her green wings. Did that mean they'd seen dragons before? That the other librarians had made it this far?

She stood on Kendriley's back, towering over the men, her dragon-scale armor glinting. Again she whispered *magné,* amplifying her voice.

"Greetings! We come in peace from the Dragon King."

One man stepped forward from the rest. He was in his early twenties, perhaps, twenty years younger than Tala.

He gestured with his hands. It took a moment to realize he was making a variant of the hand gestures used by temple scribes sworn to silence.

"You are welcome," he signed, *"though we can offer little hospitality. As you see, we are poor, and the land unforgiving."*

He spoke true. The village consisted of thatched hovels sprouting like mushrooms along a single muddy street. The place smelled of rot, and she twitched her nose in unease.

Still, it would be rude to say so. She climbed down from Kendriley's back. Her boots splashed on the muddy ground. "Be at ease. We're not here for your wheat or your fish. We come for your knowledge."

His expression passed from curiosity at their arrival to puzzlement when she spoke of knowledge. The men behind him proved more stony-faced, their emotions hidden behind prodigious beards.

"We are happy to help the Dragon King," the man signed. *"But what do you mean, you come for our knowledge?"*

How could he not know of the Dragon King's demands? Especially if her colleagues had come before. Was he feigning puzzlement, pretending not to know?

She answered carefully. "As repayment for the dragons putting an end to the constant warring, the King demands knowledge as part of your taxes. Since you live out so far, the librarians have been slow to reach you, but now these taxes are due."

The Beards heard this in stony silence, their faces impassive. A strange reaction, since usually people questioned her, incredulous that knowledge could be collected as a tax. Once they knew her to be in earnest, most paid gladly. Better to rebuild the libraries under a Dragon King than starve under a human lord.

In the face of impassive silence, she forged on. "You'll tell us your stories, histories, herb lore—local knowledge of any kind. All knowledge is worth collecting; nothing is outside the purview of the Library."

She paused, stymied by the unrelenting blank faces of the Beards. "In particular," she said, perhaps a bit too loudly in that silence, "we want to know what happened to our colleagues who came before us."

"We know nothing," the man signed, looking back to the Beards, *"of any colleagues who came before you."* The

Beards nodded in agreement, their heads bobbing as one.

At the sight of that silent, coordinated agreement, a shiver ran down Tala's back, under her armor. She looked away from the men, unnerved, and focused desperately on their spokesman. Was he lying? Were they all lying?

She took a breath and regretted it as the rotten smell clung to her nostrils. She gritted her teeth, swallowing down a sense of wrongness that pricked her skin. Centering her thoughts—*you're a librarian, you can gain knowledge from a grain of sand*—she tried again.

"Sola and Audrohasta came three years ago. Ko and Fenomere followed last spring. They sent word from the mainland that they were flying here, but were never heard from again. You haven't seen them?"

He blinked. She saw him make a decision. *"No."*

Liar.

Anger heated her face. Instinct urged her to reach for her dagger, made from a talon that Kendriley had lost, but reason kept her hand still. Anger wouldn't help her friends.

"You're sure?" she asked, her voice harsh. "Two of them were dragons, remember. Not as large as Kendriley, but still much larger than oxen. Hard to miss. You never saw them?"

His lips thinned. *"No."*

"I find that difficult to believe. You're sure none of you saw them?"

"I am sure."

He was more opaque than a grain of sand. Exasperated, she blew out her breath and tried a different approach. "Dragons value knowledge above all else and would pay handsomely for information about why four of their librarians vanished."

"I'm sorry," he signed. *"Some knowledge simply cannot be bought. Please, have tea before you go. The flight back will be long."*

Again, that maddening, blank silence. Tala opened her mouth, ready to scream, but Kendriley spoke: "Enough."

Tala froze. The Beards jumped. One dropped a trowel. He snatched it up, glowering at Kendriley.

Why had she spoken? She rarely did in front of those unused to dragon-speak. Then Tala smelled the rot again. Only this time it was both a stench and a sense of evil that prickled up her back. It seemed to seep from the ground, from the very core of the island, rising in response to Kendriley's voice. Kendriley shifted, as if she could no longer bear to make contact with the earth.

The Beards stared, silent still, their expressions unchanged, and Tala realized they didn't sense the evil. Either they couldn't, or they were inured to it.

She swallowed, a bitter taste in her mouth. All she could think was to get away.

To the spokesman she said, "Even if you can't tell us of our colleagues, you still owe the King your knowledge. Kendriley and I will survey the island, decide what we most want to know."

The man swept a circle with one arm. *"Look around you. We have no knowledge worth your gathering."*

"All knowledge is worth gathering."

She remounted, grateful to be back on Kendriley. Quickly, they left the men of Dreden behind.

"What *is* that feeling?" Tala asked two hours later as she fed dry wood to their campfire. Gloomy afternoon light struggled to pierce the low-hanging clouds. They had circled the island for some time, fruitlessly following one scent trail after another in search of the evil before making camp deep in the winter-bare forest. "It keeps coming and going."

"Like it's examining us, testing for weaknesses." Kendriley raised a talon from where she was incising one of her scales, recording the story of their arrival on Dreden. Her body wrapped halfway around the camp. An outcropping of rock on the other side provided a dry overhang for Tala's fire. "I've not encountered anything like this in all my long years, and I don't like it."

"I'd feel better if we were still out searching. Not sitting here."

Kendriley flicked her tail in agreement. "But I want you near me, because I'm going to See."

She said it with an elongated "S": Ssssee.

Tala's heart gave an unhappy lurch. "Now? The Beards are going to come for us, I'm sure of it."

"Not yet. They need time to stew and debate." Kendriley sheathed her talon, her incising done. "And when they come, they will tell us lies. I want information to use against them."

"I don't like having you vulnerable right now." Tala looked over her shoulder, out into the forest. A large blackbird perched in a nearby tree, one yellow eye trained on them. Curious, that. Birds usually kept a healthy distance from Kendriley. "Something out there has already overpowered two dragons."

"Neither of whom was as old or as powerful as I. And neither had a librarian like you by her side."

Tala swatted Kendriley playfully. "Now you're just talking nonsense."

"I put my life in your hands every time my mind leaves my body. I trust you'll see I have a body to return to."

Tala sobered. "Of course. You be careful."

"Cross my heart. You, too, kitling."

Which made Tala smile, as always. She held still, listening to the drips of the sodden forest, while Kendriley settled into her trance. It was unnerving to see the body of her friend grow lax and unresponsive. In that moment, Tala knew, Kendriley became both Kendriley and not-Kendriley. She inhabited both herself and the beings around her--birds, snakes, trees, rocks–-connecting herself to them so she saw what they saw and knew what they knew.

She could be minutes or hours in the trance. Best to stay busy, Tala had learned. It kept her from brooding over a dragon who looked near death.

So while her dinner cooked, she pored over Kendriley's carvings, searching for some clue they had missed. As usual, the notes were thorough, the observations recorded in precise shorthand. Beside the new notes were two incised scales ready to be shed. One came off in her hand, and she tucked it into their bags. It would join the thousands of other scales in the Dragon King's library, making a fireproof, nearly indestructible record of the kingdom's reconstructed knowledge. In its place a new scale would grow, ready for Kendriley to incise with whatever they learned next.

Tala hoped it would be the identity of whatever lurked out there. The blackbird still watched them, its feathers glistening in the rain.

"And what do you want?" Tala called.

The bird didn't respond.

Hurry up, Kendri, Tala thought. She was as jumpy as a novice at her first dragon moot.

When they were first paired together fifteen years before, Kendriley had explained the mechanics of Seeing. Tala hadn't understood it then, and she still only knew that it was an adaptation of the mindspeak all dragons used while they flew. Only the oldest and most powerful dragons dared to See. Younger, weaker minds were susceptible to being taken over.

Suddenly, Kendriley stiffened.

Tala went to her and stroked her neck scales. "Shh, it's all right. I'm here."

Kendriley groaned. The noise rumbled, deep and eerie, and the hair on Tala's arms stood on end.

"Kendri?"

Kendriley thrashed. Her tail whipped into the campsite, scattering their bags, the studded end digging into the earth. Tala scrambled back.

"Wake up!" She spun away from the spiked elbow on Kendriley's right wing. The tip scored the outcropping. "Kendri, wake up!"

Kendriley's silver eyes were open and unseeing. She pulled back her lips, baring her fangs.

"Wake up!" Tala grabbed the bucket of water from beside the fire. She sloshed Kendriley's face.

Kendriley hissed. Her gaze bored into Tala.

"Hillside," she said.

Then she slapped her front paws over her snout. Her eyes squeezed shut, and she sank down on the ground, trembling.

"Kendri?" Tala clutched her bucket, uncertain. Should she run for more water or tend Kendriley?

Kendriley didn't seem to want tending. She huddled on the ground, her tail pulled tight around her, her every muscle rigid. Instinctively, Tala knew not to touch her.

She turned instead to the outcropping of rock bordering the campsite.

Did it qualify as a hillside? Was the evil inside it? Was that why Kendriley had scored it with her wingtip? Had she meant her word as a warning or a call to act?

Tala dropped to her knees beside Kendriley's head, looking to her friend for clues. They were in short supply. Kendriley shivered, her scales prickling like a horse bothered by flies. All Tala could think was that the Seeing had gone bad. She had heard stories, of course, but never expected to witness a bad Seeing, not with Kendriley. Still, the trembling, the thrashing, the paws slapped over her snout—everything hinted that some consciousness Kendriley had entered was trying to take over hers. It seemed impossible that something could possess a dragon of her age. Surely it wasn't the sparrows and oaks she normally connected with.

Tala stood and glared into the forest. The blackbird stared back with its unblinking yellow eyes.

"Let her go," she yelled. She threw a stone, which just missed the bird's back. "Tell me what you *want*."

No response, not evening a ruffling of its feathers, only the hissing of the wind in the trees that seemed almost to whisper a word.

A half hour later, someone crashed their way through the forest. Tala sheathed her dagger from where she'd been digging into the hillside. Carefully, she planted herself between the trees and Kendriley's vulnerable head. She wished she felt more imposing without Kendriley alert behind her. She was dirty and frustrated—there had been nothing unusual about the hillside. At least the fire glinted an impressive red and yellow on her armor.

The man who had signed at her in the village stalked into view. A burlap bag hung from each shoulder, giving no indication of what good or bad things they might contain.

He walked forward carefully, his hands in plain view. The unflappable blackbird watched his approach.

He stood about twenty steps away when Tala asked, "What do you want?"

He set down the bags. *"I guessed you might camp here. My name is Bolen. I come alone, with answers to your questions."*

"You claimed not to know anything earlier." She glanced into the forest. Were the others waiting there? She needed their information, yes, but what would they do if they knew of Kendriley's vulnerability? "Prove you have answers."

"It was the elders." His face twisted in disdain as he signed of them. *"They had your friends killed."* He opened one of the bags, scooped out a handful of red and

blue scales. They were all that remained of a dragon after death.

Tala sucked in her breath. She'd known her friends might be dead, had reconciled herself to the possibility months ago. But to see the proof in his hands...

She couldn't dwell on it now. Not with Kendriley in danger. And she didn't trust this man's sudden tattling. What if he was lying again? "You're saying a group of old men took down two dragons and two trained librarians?"

"They're old, but they aren't stupid, and young dragons aren't invincible."

She could imagine it—an arrow below the jaw, or in the eye. Or a welcoming sip of poisoned tea.

"Were the elders acting on their own? Or are they under the control of the evil?"

Fear crossed his face. He swallowed.

"Tell me," she pressed. "What is the evil?"

His face went white. That, she was sure, was not a lie. *"What do you know?"*

"You tell me."

He licked his lips and pointed to Kendriley. *"Is your dragon all right?"*

"She's meditating. To increase her power." She paused to let him come to his own conclusion about that.

He eyed Kendriley as if she would eat him at any moment.

"Time's wasting," Tala said when he didn't speak. "I'd hate to think what would happen if your elders found you speaking to me."

He glanced fearfully into the forest. There, all was still. The blackbird remained silent, as if waiting to see what happened between her and this man, Bolen.

"All right," he signed. *"I'm tired of serving them. I'll tell you about the evil."* With the decision made, he seemed to stand taller. *"But I want to talk to the dragon."*

"Anything you can say to Kendriley you can say to me."

"That, librarian, is where you're wrong."

"Why am I wrong?"

His face was grim. *"Because only a dragon of her power can hope to destroy our evil."*

"You can see it best from up here," Bolen signed down to Tala.

She nodded and grabbed a clump of grass to haul herself up. Bolen scaled the incline like a mountain goat. She wondered how many times he'd made this climb.

He had signed, *"It's on a hillside,"* and that word alone had made her leave Kendriley's side. She had promised to rouse Kendriley once she was satisfied by what Bolen showed her. Now, hauling herself up, she gasped for breath and hoped there would be a Kendriley to rouse.

He didn't comment on her windedness, simply offered a hand to pull her up the last particularly steep ledge.

Wheezing, she stood on a flat tabletop of land. It gave a panoramic view of forest behind and to her left, a burned-out meadow in front of her, and soggy fields to her right. Beyond the fields, she could make out the Beards in their village square, engaged in silent, signed disagreements. Even farther over her right shoulder, Kendriley glittered green beneath the dark skeletons of trees.

Keep fighting, Kendri. I'm coming.

"Get down," Bolen signed, flattening himself to the ground. *"Let's hope it doesn't sense us here."*

Tala ducked, her armor rattling. She followed his lead as he crawled to the edge of the flat top. Below it, the ground sloped down to the burned-out meadow.

"Over there." Bolen pointed to the large hill that bordered the far side of the meadow.

She frowned, puzzled, for she and Kendriley had flown over the area earlier that afternoon. The hill was steep, though not as steep as the incline they'd just climbed. The bare, burned soil and rock showed grayish brown in the afternoon sun. Except now it became obvious that not all of the hill was rock or soil. A wooden panel the size of a large door lay across the face of the hill. It had been painted to blend in with the earth.

As she stared at that panel, dread churned her belly. It was the evil she'd sensed before, rising now as if summoned by Bolen's signing and her gaze. Only now it was stronger, more concentrated, and she had no doubt that whatever it was emanated from behind that panel. She breathed between her teeth to keep from flinching.

"What's behind there?"

Bolen gave her a look of undiluted terror. He hunched down, keeping his hands out of view of the hill. *"A Word."*

She gaped. Her heart thudded in a confused, animal terror. "But Words alone —they have no power."

"Quiet!" He threw a glance at the panel. His face went grey. *"Look out! Stop your ears! Don't listen!"*

Only a flock of birds flew over the meadow. "Wha—?"

Bolen pressed his hands over her ears. As he did, the birds descended, cawing. The sound was harsh, unbird-like. It grated against her ears, sent shivers down her spine. She slapped her hands over Bolen's and screamed a minor Word to deaden sound.

It helped, but the sound still battered against her ears. It wormed down her throat and up her nose, searching, striving to reach her mind. "No," she whispered, filling her mind with her own voice. "No. No. No."

The attack seemed to go on forever, but must have been only moments. Then the birds soared away, and Bolen released her.

They were both panting. Bolen's lips moved as if he wanted to make a sound but couldn't. Tala wiped her mouth, tasting blood. She must have bitten her tongue.

"What was that?" she demanded.

He shook his head. He motioned back the way they'd come. *"Not here."*

He crawled across the flat top and started down. Tala eyed the hillside, her stomach twisting. The panel looked unchanged, the sky clear of birds. She followed. She didn't stop until they were back among the trees on level ground.

"Talk to me," she said. Even in her armor she felt vulnerable. "What just happened?"

Bolen rubbed his beard. He breathed heavily, the sound labored, though he hadn't on the climb up. Scratches marred the backs of his hands. Tala realized she must have made them.

"There's a Word, an evil Word, carved into that hill. It just tried to get you to hear it so you would speak it."

"By sending birds to caw at me?"

"They're mimics. The Word takes over their minds, makes them speak."

Kendriley, she thought with a shiver. She wished she could see the dragon's comforting glitter.

"Did you carve this Word, you and the elders?"

"No! We're the guardians. It's our job to make sure it remains hidden, unknown and unspoken."

"And it made you kill my friends?"

He shook his head, rubbing at his scratches. *"They—we—did that. Your friends had to die, so they wouldn't bring knowledge of the Word to the Library."*

She forced herself to speak calmly. "You don't have to kill anyone. Just chisel the Word off the hillside. "

He gaped as if she were mad. *"You think we haven't tried that? It can't be chiseled off. It can't be scorched off. We've painted over it, tried to grow plants to break the hill apart. Nothing works. We have to replace the panel every year. The best we can do is achieve a stalemate, but you librarians came and threatened the balance."*

"You killed your best chance." She would have laughed if it weren't so important. "We don't just collect knowledge. Some librarians are scholars who specialize in words and magic. They could help you."

He shook his head. *"No one must learn of it. Some things are better left unknown."*

"Everything is worth knowing. Look what happened when the wars destroyed the libraries. The land fell into chaos. I promise the scholars will help."

"And have every power-mad idiot flocking here, hoping to use it for their own ends?" He shuddered. *"I want your promise that Kendriley will obliterate it. Her fire must be hot enough, or her claws sharp enough."*

Tala looked him full in the face. He was wrong. Only by knowing something could you face it. "What does it do?" she asked, enunciated each word clearly.

"Destroy." He made the sign with a swipe of his hand. *"It gives the speaker power to kill, to obliterate, to dismantle anything at a word."*

"Why would it want to do that?"

"It's a Word. It does what it was created to do. Our legends say the magician who created it sought the ultimate secret—to revive the stillborn baby born to his grieving wife. But such knowledge is not for humans, and it drove him mad. When he couldn't create, he

vowed to destroy. If the Word took possession of someone powerful enough, it could destroy the world."

"Powerful   enough—Oh,   gods, Kendriley." No wonder she had slapped her paws over her snout. She was fighting for the life of everything on earth.

Bolen frowned. *"What?"*

"We have to get to Kendriley." She ran, sprinting towards the campsite. Fear was like a wind at her back.

Hold on, Kendri.

With Bolen beside her, Tala thundered into the clearing. Kendriley still huddled there. Tala gave a silent prayer of thanks to see her alive and--

"Oh, gods." She ran to Kendriley's side. "Her tail's gone."

Kendriley's tail ended in a stump about an arm's length from her body. The end oozed, raw and seeping. The air stank of blood. A mound of scales showed where she'd tucked her tail close to her belly.

"It must have forced her to speak," Tala whispered, her hand at her throat. "She destroyed part of herself rather than anything else."

"It's already taken her over." Bolen glared at Tala. *"What hope is there now of stopping it? You should've told me earlier."*

She'd gasped the story out during their race to the campsite. Now she glared back as she ransacked their bags. Nothing was big enough for a bandage. "And you should've told us right away about the Word. She's still fighting, so help me find some way to help her, or shut up."

Bolen sank down on his haunches. *"Nothing can help her. She was the only chance we had."*

"Shut up." She threw down their last bag and kicked it. "No, wait." She rounded on him. "How do you lot resist it?"

Something like pride made him stiffen. *"We drink a brew every morning. In time, it destroys our voices. The Word knows we can never speak it."*

No wonder the Beards had been silent. She had a new respect for the villagers of Dreden, even if they were murderers. But that method was too slow. Kendriley didn't have time to gradually lose her voice. "What about before the potion works?"

"If the Word seems too strong in a youngster, we cut out their tongue."

Her jaw dropped. She snapped it shut.

"It's better than speaking the Word." He shoved up his left sleeve. *"We also mark ourselves with this."* It was a minor Word —*defendé*—carved into the skin of his forearm. *"I don't know what it means. None of us read."*

"It's an ancient protective Word."

With that, an idea formed. Tala's heart thudded.

"It stops working after a while."

"Yes," she said idly, staring at his scar. "For true protection, you'd need to carve a major Word of power."

"I—" Bolen signed, but Tala strode past him. She knelt by Kendriley's head. Cautiously, she placed one hand on Kendriley's left paw, where it was still wrapped about her snout. Kendriley shook like a bowstring.

"I know what you're fighting," Tala said softly. "I saw the hillside."

Kendriley opened one eye. Her gaze held pain and urgency.

Tala swallowed back tears. "I know lots of Words, minor and major ones, but I don't know any with power great enough to protect you. What's the greatest protective Word you know?"

Kendriley growled deep in her throat. Bolen started, backing away.

Tala merely shook her head. "I don't understand. What?"

Kendriley growled again. Tala felt it in her palm. There was a word in the growl, buried deep in dragon-speech.

"One more time. Please." She bent down, placed her ear next to Kendriley's lips.

Kendriley growled, Tala strained her ears, and the forest erupted with deafening bird caws. It wasn't the grating sound of before. There was no single insistent word, still the noise overpowered Kendriley's voice.

"Quiet!" Tala screamed.

Silence descended.

For Kendriley, too. She trembled in mute battle.

"No." Tala shook her. "I didn't mean you. What Word should I use?"

Kendriley didn't respond.

Bolen touched Tala's elbow. *"See? It's too powerful."*

She yanked her elbow back. In that moment, she wished him and his Word a hundred thousand leagues away. "I'm going to carve a protective Word on her."

"What good will that do? She's already possessed."

"If I can find a Word of great enough power, it'll let her regain her own mind. Then she can See. She can re-connect with the Word but not be overpowered by it."

His face lit up. *"Does this mean she can speak the Word against itself? Force it to destroy itself?"*

Tala nodded. She pressed her forehead against Kendriley's side, breathing in her smoky smell.

"Oh." He had worked out the hitch in the plan. *"But you just said—She'll be Seeing, so she'll be connected to the Word. In destroying it, she'll destroy herself."*

"Damn you, Kendri," Tala whispered, because she knew she had no choice, and she hated that knowing.

Bolen rose to his feet. *"I could do the carving if you show me what symbols—"*

"No." She pushed herself up. "Kendriley is my friend. You keep watch. Tell me if that overgrown noun so much as makes a splinter in its panel."

"Of course. Good luck." He climbed the outcropping that made up one side of the camp. As easily as if it were a set of stairs, he pulled himself up over the crown of the trees. *"I can just see the panel,"* he signed down.

Tala took a deep breath. She rested one hand on Kendriley's head, feeling the ridges of the scales, the warmth of them under her palm. Then she pulled out her talon knife. She found the slight break in scales where she'd harvested one that afternoon. Using her knife, she prized off four of the neighboring scales. Kendriley shuddered. Blood the color of wine streamed down her exposed skin.

"I'm sorry." Tala pressed her hand to the wounds, holding until the hot blood slowed to a trickle. The bare spot looked horrible, but the damage would be worth it to give Kendrily the full protective power of carving on skin rather than scales.

Only one Word she knew could possibly hold more power than the one on the hillside. She'd last invoked it before the examination to enter the Library.

She whispered a prayer and began to carve.

COG

The ground shook. A tree cracked, and a branch the width of her leg crashed down behind her. Tala gritted her teeth, bracing an arm against Kendriley's side.

COGNIT

Kendriley roared, part triumph, part pain.

Birds swarmed around Tala. They mobbed her, their feathers sticking against her eyes, her nose. She couldn't see, couldn't breathe. She choked, suffocating under the smell of rot.

By feel alone she carved: COGNITIÉ.

A crack, as if the world had split open. Tala found herself on the ground, in a swirl of feathers, her knife still clutched in her fist.

Kendriley growled. Her tail thrashed, scattering birds. Her growl rumbled through the earth, loud, but just a growl. There was no Word in it.

"The panel cracked," Bolen signed, barely visible through a mass of birds. *"But the Word's still there. Your plan isn't working."*

Tala spit out feathers, gasping for air. What else could she do?

She scrambled onto her knees as Kendriley writhed, her paws still over her snout. Blood dripped from the carved letters. If one Word was too weak, would two work? But what other Word would do? No other Word of power—

No.

Tala gasped.

She didn't need a Word of power.

She staggered to her feet, her knees shaking.

This Word would not submit to more power. But she had a secret weapon: She knew the history of this Word, while it knew next to nothing about her. Knowledge could save them all.

"Hurry!" Bolen signed.

Kendriley's head drooped lower. Her tail flopped. She could not struggle much longer.

Frantically, Tala stumbled to her. She grabbed one of Kendriley's ears. The scales were warm under her fingers.

Once chance. What one fact, one utterance would distract the Word? Allow Kendriley the moment she needed to See?

She closed her eyes, crossed her fingers, prayed that the myth of the grieving magician held a kernel of truth, a nugget that spoke of true knowledge.

She whispered not a Word of power, but a powerful word: "Creation."

The ground shook. Kendriley roared. The Word was lost in the roar, which rumbled in Tala's spine and molars. Her ears rang. She sat down sharply.

The birds flew away, disappearing into the forest. On the outcropping, Bolen jumped up and down. *"It's gone!"* he signed. *"The panel fell away, and there's nothing but ruined earth behind it. You did it!"*

We did it, Tala thought, and though she was afraid to, she turned her head.

Kendrily lay on her side, breathing shallowly, her eyes tightly closed.

Tala laid a hand on Kendriley's snout. "You're alive."

Kendriley slit open an eye. Her lips curled in a dragon smile.

"Thanks to you, kitling. But not for long. The protective power is fading."

"No! You're not going to die."

Kendriley winced. "Yes, I am. And before I do, you must promise me. Tell no one of the Word. Let all knowledge of it pass from this earth."

"I can't. You know that. We must collect what we've learned."

"Oh, kitling. Being a librarian isn't all about collecting knowledge. Sometimes you have to discard it, too."

"Never. Lost knowledge only leads to chaos."

Kendriley growled. "I've already alerted the other dragons of my passing. When they come, they mustn't gain knowledge of the Word. Don't let me die in vain."

"No!" Tears pricked Tala's eyes. "There must be another way."

"There isn't. If knowledge of the Word survives, my sacrifice will mean nothing. Promise me, kitling, that my death will mean something."

Desperately, Tala stroked Kendriley's snout. She wanted to deny it, to cling to her certainty that knowledge must be preserved above all else. But how could she deny Kendriley her dying wish?

Finally, she nodded. "Cross my heart."

"Thank you." Kendriley closed her eyes. Her body quivered. Then it vanished. Her scales tinkled as they collapsed, leaving a dragon-shaped mound along one edge of the campsite.

Tala shook. Before long, the dragons would arrive. They would arrange for the islanders to face the King's justice and for Tala to return to the Library.

So now, alone in the late afternoon sun, surrounded by scales and feathers, Tala picked up a blank scale. It was still warm and smelled of dragon. With her dagger, she carved a false version of what had happened, omitting all mention of the Word.

She wept as she carved, the tears leaking salt into her mouth. They dropped onto the scale, making it glitter like glass, sharp and smooth and deceptively bright.

When she was done, she set down her dagger and wrapped her arms around herself, holding tight as she rocked. Carving the scale had been her last act as a librarian. She would not pick up another dragon-talon dagger. That decision was simple. She would never again serve as a librarian, not when it meant hiding the truth of Kendriley's death. For truth could be kept from the world, but not from herself.

About the story

I'm honestly trying to remember what inspired this story. Perhaps my recollection is faulty, but I remember coming home from World Fantasy 2014 with the idea for a dragon-library. Perhaps I got the idea while attending a panel? I can't remember. But the idea for a dragon-library stuck, and then it was a matter of trying to make a dragon-library into a story. It took me a while to figure out that the library was composed of information recorded on dragon scales, but once I knew that, the story grew. Of course, as a librarian, I really, really want a dragon for my own library.

A question for the author

Q: What's easier for you - imagining a happier world, or a darker one?

A: If we're talking about a future for our own world, sadly it's easier for me to think that this world will get darker, at least in the immediate future. However, if we're talking about an imaginary story world, then it's easier for me to imagine a happier one. I write and I read fantasy to experience places unlike the world I inhabit every day. Why not make those happier ones?

About the author

Kathryn Yelinek works as a librarian in Pennsylvania. In addition to the required hobbies of reading and writing, she enjoys bird watching, star-gazing, gardening, and going to see Broadway musicals. She and her fiancé share their home with two parakeets, whom they are actively striving to make into the most spoiled birds in the Western Hemisphere. The birds don't seem to mind. Her work has appeared or is forthcoming in *Daily Science Fiction, Deep Magic, Metaphorosis, Andromeda Spaceways Magazine,* and *Beneath Ceaseless Skies.*

kathrynyelinek.com

Suzy's Friend

David Hammond

From: gruntbuggly54@gmail.com
To: shanover@fnal.gov
Subject: Water temperature

Dear Dr. Hanover,

I am writing on behalf of the *Octopus bimaculoides* in your office aquarium whom you call Suzy. The water is too warm. Please reduce the temperature to 18℃. She would greatly appreciate it.

Sincerely,

Suzy's Friend

From: shanover@fnal.gov
To: gruntbuggly54@gmail.com
Subject: Re: Water temperature

I don't know who you are, and this is obviously some kind of joke, but the funny thing is that I tested the water and found that it was indeed too warm and that my thermostat was broken. I have replaced the thermostat and set it to the proper temperature (20°C).

Cheers and thanks for the unwitting help.

Best Regards,

Steve

P.S. I have changed the lock on my office door and alerted security. I assure you that if you return you will be caught and prosecuted to the full extent of the law. Unless this is Fawad, in which case I will personally wring your neck.

From: gruntbuggly54@gmail.com
To: shanover@fnal.gov
Subject: Re: Water temperature

Dear Dr. Hanover,

Suzy and I thank you for your efforts in replacing the thermostat, but would you be so kind as to reduce the temperature to 18°C as I originally requested? Suzy prefers cooler waters. Suzy promises to solve the bottle/ring puzzle for you if you do her this small favor.

Sincerely,

Suzy's Friend

From: shanover@fnal.gov
To: gruntbuggly54@gmail.com
Subject: Re: Water temperature

Okay, I have to admit that I deleted your last email initially, but then I couldn't stop thinking about it. I just can't understand how you know about the bottle/ring puzzle. Last night I reduced the temperature on the tank, and in the morning I gave Suzy the puzzle, and she attacked it right away. She solved it in under 30 seconds. Incredible. She had not gotten close before.

So, all I can say is *bravo!* This is one heck of a practical joke. I don't know how you did it, but you got me.

Oh my god! I just realized that your email address is a reference to *The Hitchhiker's Guide to the Galaxy!* "Oh freddled gruntbuggly, thy micturations are to me..." This is Colleen, isn't it? You're the

only person I know who would quote
Vogon poetry! You're very good.

Mordiously yours,

Steve

From: gruntbuggly54@gmail.com
To: shanover@fnal.gov
Subject: Re: Water temperature

Dear Dr. Hanover,

Thank you so much for adjusting the
temperature!

We hesitate to ask, but Suzy would like to
have a bigger tank, though we of course
realize that it may be beyond your means.
If money is an object, we may be able to
provide funds if you can arrange for
purchasing and installing the tank. If you
agree, Suzy will happily solve any puzzle
you like. 200 gallons would be great, but
the bigger the better.

By now, perhaps, you have interrogated
Colleen and know that I am not she. You
do not know me. I am not a thief nor a
practical joker. I am simply, and always,

Sincerely,

Suzy's Friend

From: shanover@fnal.gov
To: gruntbuggly54@gmail.com
Subject: Re: Water temperature

Finally cutting to the chase? I have to admit that your approach is more original than pretending to be a Nigerian prince, but come on.

From: gruntbuggly54@gmail.com
To: shanover@fnal.gov
Subject: Re: Water temperature

Dear Dr. Hanover,

I have taken the liberty of locating a 325-gallon aquarium that should do nicely. Please take a look and let me know if you have any alternative suggestions:

http://www.aquariumemporium.com/products/tidal325

And to demonstrate that I am in no way trying to perpetrate a Nigerian prince style scam, I have transferred $10,000 to your checking account, which should cover the cost of the aquarium, as well as professional installation, new filtration equipment, decorations, etc.

Let me know what you think.

Sincerely,

Suzy's Friend

From: shanover@fnal.gov
To: gruntbuggly54@gmail.com
Subject: Re: Water temperature

Who the hell are you?! The bank says the
money came from Switzerland. Of course.
I'm a little freaked out over here. Can you
understand that? Suzy's acting funny.
She keeps watching me, watching me.

Look, I'll take you at your word. You are
Suzy's friend. Okay. So if you want me to
buy this tank for her, tell me who you are,
and no more messing around.

From: gruntbuggly54@gmail.com
To: shanover@fnal.gov
Subject: Re: Water temperature

Dear Dr. Hanover,

I understand that you are "freaked out." It
is not my intention or desire to cause you
distress. The simple reason that I have
not told you more about who I am is that
you are unlikely to believe me. I have
talked this over with the others, however,
and we have decided that I might as well
tell you. It has to happen sooner or later.

My ancestors came from a planet that circles a star in the vicinity of Vega (as observed from Earth). You will no doubt be surprised to learn that we came here over 12,000 years ago but our representatives have spent most of that time in the deep ocean, in communication with a species of highly intelligent cephalopod that is, apparently, still completely unknown to humans.

It was only 50 years ago that we became more interested in the habits and cultures of land-dwelling animals on Earth. To you this must seem strange, but our home planet has no land, so it is to some extent understandable that we were largely dismissive of creatures that had abandoned the rich ocean environment to scuttle and scramble on the parched land. I admit that we were ignorant. We have since come to appreciate the bizarre and interesting lives of land animals, especially humans. In fact, in the last 10-20 years we have made a concerted effort to learn human languages. It has been an extraordinarily difficult task, let me tell you. We found the cephalopod mode of communication much easier to learn. But we have now, I am proud to say, a number of excellent translators able to work in human English as well as Chinese, Spanish and Hindi. I am, of course, working with one to translate my correspondence with you.

We were at first shocked and dismayed to see that some of our cephalopod brethren were imprisoned by humans in glass cages, with barely enough room to move, and fed restricted diets of subpar food. Some among us even advocated for punitive retaliation against humans and their societies. Fortunately, calmer minds prevailed, and we embarked instead on a program of surreptitious liberation of the cephalopods. You may recall hearing about some high-profile disappearances of octopuses from public aquariums a few years back. That was us.

Along the way, we began to see that many of the human captors were actually very well-meaning, and that many of the captive cephalopods were loath to leave what they considered their homes. And so we further moderated our strategy to, where appropriate, improve the living conditions of some cephalopods without removing them outright.

And that brings us to Suzy, who has a certain fondness for you and a sincere, though in my view unwarranted, dread of the open ocean.

I hope this goes some way in satisfying your curiosity about my identity. My translator tells me that my name would be impossible to render in English, and so I remain,

Sincerely,

Suzy's Friend

P.S. Have you had a chance to review the details of the new aquarium? That link again:

http://www.aquariumemporium.com/products/tidal325

From: gruntbuggly54@gmail.com
To: shanover@fnal.gov
Subject: Re: Water temperature
Attachment: currents.dat

Dear Dr. Hanover,

I am unsure how to interpret your silence since my last email. The most likely explanation is that you think I am an insane person, or that I am "trolling" you, or both.

A colleague of mine came up with a clever way to convince you that I am telling the truth, considering that you are a scientist.

If you or someone you know can point a radio telescope to the coordinates RA:18h35m72.6s   Dec:+38°47'11.3" tonight from 22:03:45.875 to 22:05:22.378 UTC, you will be able to detect a data pattern that matches the pattern in the attached file.

Without getting into too much detail, this is a transmission from our planet, a sort of patriotic song, if you will, to which we like to hum. It helps connect us to home.

Sincerely,

Suzy's Friend

From: shanover@fnal.gov
To: bcho@seti.org
Subject: Time-sensitive Target

Ben,

Sorry for the short notice, but can SETI collect data from the following coordinates tonight? I know you're mostly retired, but you still pull some weight in Mountain View, don't you?

It's probably nothing, but if it's something, it's huge.

RA:18h35m72.6s Dec:+38°47'11.3"
22:03:45.875 - 22:05:22.378 UTC

Steve

From: bcho@seti.org
To: shanover@fnal.gov
Subject: Re: Time-sensitive Target
Attachment: 4steve.dat

Had to pull strings to get telescope time. Quick analysis shows nothing but noise. What were you hoping to find? You owe me a beer. Two beers. Mmmmmm, beer.

Ben

From: shanover@fnal.gov
To: bcho@seti.org
Subject: Re: Time-sensitive Target

Ben,

You guys may need to redefine what you call noise.

I have to shop for a new aquarium this weekend. Join me? I will explain my above enigmatic comment. I'm on to something big. Huge. Better than beer.

Steve

P.S. Will also provide beer.

From: shanover@fnal.gov
To: gruntbuggly54@gmail.com
Subject: Re: Water temperature

Dear Suzy's Friend,

The new aquarium is installed and Suzy seems quite happy in it, though due to the increased size the water will take a little while to condition properly.

I have so many questions I don't know where to start! I am just going to ask them as they occur to me. I apologize in advance for the barrage. A friend of mine who works with SETI, Ben Cho, is here too. He is even more excited than I am, as you can imagine.

What do you look like? How have you remained hidden from us for so long, even while learning our languages? Are you able to disguise yourselves as humans? Have you been living among us or do you observe us from afar?

How do you communicate with Suzy, or perhaps more to the point, how does she communicate with you? Have you planted some sort of communication device in her tank? (None was found in the aquarium transfer.) Does she do it visually with variations in skin tone, and if so how do you see that?

Please tell us more about the highly-intelligent cephalopods in our oceans! We would very much like to meet them and communicate with them. Would you be willing to translate for us?

Are there other advanced species like you in the universe that you know of? How many? We have often thought that there must be millions of advanced civilizations in our galaxy alone, but since we have never met any of them there has been a great deal of doubt and debate on this subject.

Tell us about your space ships! How fast can they travel and what do they use for propulsion? As water-dwellers, how did you even make the leap into space in the first place?

Tell us about your civilization! What form of government, if any, do you have? Have you dealt with self-made existential threats such as nuclear weapons and rapid climate change? If so, how? Is there hope for us in the long run?

Any responses to the above questions would be greatly appreciated. We are eager to learn from you, cooperate with you, and help you in any way we can.

Sincerely,

Steven Hanover

From: mailer-daemon@googlemail.com
To: shanover@fnal.gov
Subject: Delivery Status Notification
(Failure)

Your message wasn't delivered to
gruntbuggly54@gmail.com because the
address couldn't be found. Check for
typos or unnecessary spaces and try
again.

From: bcho@seti.org
To: shanover@fnal.gov
Subject: Search for the Vogon Poet

Checked with my friend at Google and no
luck tracing the emails.

I sent the data to Sharon, and she
thought it was interesting but was
skeptical. Laughed at me actually. It
stung. Agreed to continue monitoring
Vogon, but for a limited time.

Still sure it's not a clever joke?

Ben

From: suzyeightlegs@gmail.com
To: shanover@fnal.gov
Subject: Greetings

Hello, this is Suzy! I like the new aquarium very much, but the water tastes weird!

More live food, please! I like to catch the shrimp. It is so fun and they taste good.

I like to solve puzzles.

What do you like?

Why did you put me in a tank in your office?

Why do you turn off the lights and sit in the dark and watch me for so long?

Where do you go at night?

If you write back, the translator will translate for me. The translator is nice!

From: shanover@fnal.gov
To: suzyeightlegs@gmail.com
Subject: Re: Greetings

Dear Suzy,

I was so happy to get your email, you have no idea! I'm glad that you like the new aquarium. I like it too. Hopefully the water will taste better soon, and I will keep the shrimp coming!

I will attempt to answer your questions.

I like to look at the stars. I have a big telescope and I use it to look deep into the universe. I like to imagine traveling out in space and exploring new worlds. I like to learn new things.

I put you in a tank in my office because I had always wanted an octopus as a pet. I knew that octopuses were very intelligent, though I never imagined writing an email to one! I also just wanted something pretty in my office to look at. When I am bored, or just need to think, I turn off the lights and watch you in your tank, and it is soothing to my mind.

At night I go to a house a few miles from the office, and, mostly, I sleep. I dream about mathematical equations, and I dream about distant planets. I dream about you sometimes, and sometimes you talk to me and tell me that I am a silly human.

Do you dream, Suzy?

I have a favor to ask. When I come in tomorrow morning, I will drop the blue bottle in the end of the tank by the window. Please pick it up, move it to the other side of the tank and drop it there. That's all! If you do this, I will know that you received this message, and then I will give you some shrimp.

Love,

Steve

From: shanover@fnal.gov
To: bcho@seti.org
Subject: Re: Search for the Vogon Poet

I'm sure. Call me.

Steve

From: suzyeightlegs@gmail.com
To: shanover@fnal.gov
Subject: Re: Greetings

The translator had to explain to me the concept of "dream," because I never thought about it before. But yes, I do!

I like to rest under the purple coral, and then I go on trips. That is how I have always thought about it. And sometimes I go to the ocean too, and some of these trips are very scary. It is why I don't like the ocean, even though I've never been there!

My friend—not the translator, the other one—told me that the ocean is interesting and full of good things to eat, but it is

very, very big, and that's the thing that
worries me.

From: shanover@fnal.gov
To: suzyeightlegs@gmail.com
Subject: Re: Greetings

Dear Suzy,

We have something in common! I am also
afraid of the ocean, of how big it is. I went
scuba diving in the ocean once, and it was
as beautiful and interesting as your friend
says. When I looked at things up close—
the coral, the fish, the anemones—it was
pleasant and fascinating, but when I
peered ahead of me into that seemingly
endless expanse of dark water I felt
unmoored and overwhelmed.

Was it the creatures that may lurk there
that frightened me, or was it the sheer
size? Would I feel the same terror floating
out in space?

Anyway, to think that some of those
creatures may be like you comforts me,
and makes me want to try scuba diving
again!

I would like to ask the translator
something. Can I talk to you? We have
been given such a tantalizing glimpse of a

world beyond our understanding. I repeat that we want to learn from you, cooperate with you, and help you in any way we can.

Sincerely,

Steve

From: irfan.bashir@noaa.gov
To: shanover@fnal.gov
Subject: Wow

Couldn't sleep after your call. That's some crazy shit. Mind blown.

I don't know if I made it clear last night, I was so stunned, but if you can't narrow down the search area then NOAA can do exactly nothing. Nada. Zip. Zilch. Even if you can narrow it down, funds are tight and it will take some political jujitsu to get an expedition in the water. Keeping it real.

Damn that's exciting though. You better not be messing with me. Keep me in the loop.

Irfan

From: suzyeightlegs@gmail.com
To: shanover@fnal.gov
Subject: Re: Greetings

If you are afraid of the ocean too, then I don't feel so bad. I would like to see you scuba diving. It would be so funny!

The translator says that she is professional and is only supposed to translate for me. She told me to tell you that, and she is sorry.

By the way, I talk to the translator when I go on my trips (dream, you call it). She tells me your message and I tell her what to tell you. She reminds me a bit of a shrimp, but much bigger, and I wonder why she doesn't mind that I eat shrimp. She says it is because life is cruel, but I don't understand that explanation at all.

But unlike a shrimp her legs are long and on the end of each she has something like a human hand. She is constantly doing things with her hands—busy, busy, busy—even when she is listening to me. She rides a machine of some sort, and her hands fly around the machine pushing and pulling and poking things. I don't know what she's doing. She comes and goes on the machine so quickly it frightens me, but I am getting used to it.

So that is the translator you are so curious about. And my other friend is like her, only older, I think, because he looks ragged at the edges and moves slower.

From: shanover@fnal.gov
To: bcho@seti.org
Cc: irfan.bashir@noaa.gov
Subject: Re: Search for the Vogon Poet

Any news?

Steve

From: bcho@seti.org
To: shanover@fnal.gov
Cc: irfan.bashir@noaa.gov
Subject: Re: Search for the Vogon Poet

The data are weird. The "song" pops up at random times, but otherwise can't find a pattern.

I think I'm going crazy. Yesterday I lowered the frequency and fed the data into an audio renderer. Listened for a while and fell asleep in my chair. I dreamed of giant shrimp. So vivid. One gave me a thumbs up. Do shrimp have thumbs? Yeah, I'm going crazy.

Ben

From: jim@biggsrigs.com
To: shanover@fnal.gov
Subject: Your reservation

Steve,

Your reservation is confirmed for Jan. 13 - 16. Thank you for your prompt payment! The Kraken will be gassed, equipped, and ready to go. Howell's Dock, slip 42, any time after 7am.

Best Regards,

Jim Bigg

~~~~~ Release the Kraken! ~~~~~

From: shanover@fnal.gov
To: sales@biggsrigs.com
Subject: Re: Your reservation

Hi, Jim. Looks like you got the wrong email address. I didn't reserve anything.

From: suzyeightlegs@gmail.com
To: shanover@fnal.gov
Subject: Re: Greetings

I am so excited that we are going to the ocean! I am a little scared but mostly excited.

My friend says to tell you that you will receive a package containing a special traveling aquarium, and you can put me right in that. It will look small to you, but it will be comfortable enough for the trip.

He reserved a boat for us, but you should already know about that, he said. The captain knows where to go.

He also said that you may not want to take me, but I hope you will. Please?

From: shanover@fnal.gov
To: sales@biggsrigs.com
Subject: Re: Your reservation

Hi, Jim.

Sorry! Never mind! I don't know how I could have forgotten about the reservation. See you tomorrow.

Steve

From: sales@biggsrigs.com
To: shanover@fnal.gov
Subject: Re: Your reservation

Okay, great! See you then.

~~~~~ *Release the Kraken!* ~~~~~

From: shanover@fnal.gov
To: bcho@seti.org, irfan.bashir@noaa.gov

Attachment: itinerary.pdf
Subject: URGENT: Pack your bags

Hi, guys

Can you fly to San Diego tonight? Ben, you're not crazy. I think the giant shrimp are the Vogons and we may be able to meet them. Pack for four days on a boat. I'm bringing Suzy.

You gotta see this traveling aquarium they sent me. Whatever's in it looks like water, but it's a fraction of the weight. Some kind of sealing mechanism I can't understand. Wish I could study it more but no time!

Attaching my itinerary with hotel details. Can brief you more tonight. If you come. You've gotta come.

Steve

From: bcho@seti.org
To: shanover@fnal.gov,
irfan.bashir@noaa.gov
Subject: Re: URGENT: Pack your bags

Can't come. Please tell me what's going on. Call me from the hotel.

From: lbanafort@fnal.gov
To: staff@fnal.gov
Subject: Steven Hanover

Dear Colleagues,

It grieves me very much to say that on Friday Steven Hanover was lost at sea off the coast of San Diego and is presumed dead.

We are heartbroken, but also deeply concerned by the mysterious circumstances of Steven's ocean voyage. He left quite suddenly for San Diego, and many people have noted his strange behavior in recent weeks. He has been spending many late nights at the office and has alluded on several occasions to alarming communications he has received in email.

Steven's friend, Irfan Bashir, was on the boat with him, but returned unharmed, as did the captain of the boat, and the boat itself. All of this adds to the mystery. If anyone has any information regarding any of this, let me know, or if you think it is appropriate you may contact the San Diego PD at (619) 531-2000. They have opened an investigation into the matter.

Steven is survived by his brother Mark and his daughter Mary Pinkerton. We have sent flowers on behalf of Fermilab, and we will forward information about services as soon as they become available to us.

Sincerely,

Laura

From: bcho@seti.org
To: irfan.bashir@noaa.gov
Subject: Steve

Irfan, what happened? Nothing I've heard makes any sense.

Ben

From: irfan.bashir@noaa.gov
To: bcho@seti.org
Subject: Re: Steve

They took him, Ben. The giant shrimp with the thumbs. That's all I can figure.

We had been out for a day, heading WSW. Jim (the captain) had some gps coordinates he was aiming for. There was a storm, but it was nothing. Jim waved it off. I waved it off. Wouldn't even call it a storm, just some clouds. We put on rain gear.

Then while it was raining the wind picked up and this freak wave came along, huge and at an angle to the other waves somehow. Jim couldn't get the boat turned fast enough, so we held on and the water swept over the deck. Next thing we knew Steve was in the water. He drifted fast, too fast.

We spent three days searching. Coast Guard too.

I've been on the water a lot, and this wasn't normal. They took him. That's all I can figure.

Octopus gone too.

Irfan

From: bcho@seti.org
To: irfan.bashir@noaa.gov
Subject: Re: Steve

I listened to Vogon last night. Saw shrimp again and yelled at them in full-on spit-flecked dream rage.

They were exactly like they always are, holding up their thumbs. I think this is the message to the universe they are broadcasting. At first it seemed friendly, but now sinister. Maybe it's an insult? Maybe they are just displaying their opposable thumbs? (Universal feature of technologically advanced civilizations, maybe?) Maybe it doesn't mean anything at all?

From: irfan.bashir@noaa.gov
To: bcho@seti.org
Subject: Re: Steve

Holy shit.

http://www.sandiegouniontribune.com/breaking/hanover-found-alive.html

From: shanover@fnal.gov
To: bcho@seti.org, irfan.bashir@noaa.gov
Subject: My Trip

What a weird day at work yesterday! I felt like a celebrity, but like a celebrity that just got picked up for drunk driving and had a particularly hideous mugshot in the tabloids.

I promised I'd tell you what really happened. I woke up early for work this morning, and my mind is racing, so I may as well get into it. I'll tell it to you exactly as I remember it.

So, I had a strange feeling as the storm approached. Jim and Irfan just chided me for not taking a Dramamine, and I laughed along, but I could tell it wasn't ordinary landlubber queasiness. I brought Suzy up from the hold, and we kept each other company. As the rain got heavier, I looked out at the roiling ocean and held up Suzy so she could see.

Then the wave came, picked us up, Suzy and me, and carried us into the water. I'm an okay swimmer, so once I got over the shock of being thrust into the ocean, I collected myself and looked for the boat, but it was unaccountably far away. Suzy's ultra-light traveling aquarium floated nicely, fortunately, so I held on to it and waited, but the boat just got further away.

In about 10 minutes the boat was gone. I clung to Suzy, who seemed calm and inquisitive, looking out the bottom of her aquarium. In all directions water, a light rain falling, and I began to shiver. I was not only lost at sea, not only intimidated in my usual way by the vast expanse of water, but on top of that I was filled with the anticipation of an imminent arrival. A creature from above or below, from deep space or deep sea, with suspect motives and outlandish anatomy. I felt it approaching.

But nobody came. The sky cleared, and the sun dried my hair stiff, and I considered the other very real possibility that we were simply lost at sea, and I would die of thirst, exposure, or drowning. How long could I hold on to the aquarium? It was not a convenient floatation device. I tried to flop on top of it, but balance was precarious, and it had the tendency to flip over.

I considered Suzy, and realized that before I perished I would need to release her so that she could survive. This was, in fact, her natural habitat, or close to it. The water was roughly 18℃. I had to release her while I had the capacity to do so, though once I did the aquarium would sink, and I would perish all the sooner.

I discussed the dilemma with Suzy, scraping my words out of my parched throat. I asked her if she would like to try living in the ocean. She seemed to understand, and by gesture seemed to say that she would. I began to feel faint and feared that I might pass out, so I started fumbling with the silvery latch on the upper edge of the aquarium, my fingers numb and stuff. When I finally got the aquarium open, I rolled it over in the water. The impossibly light aquarium "water" flowed out and spread like an oil slick. Suzy dove down and undulated her legs experimentally. In a moment she was spinning joyfully. "The water tastes good!" I think she was saying.

I laughed dryly, but soon had to contend with my situation, as I quickly tired of treading water and the aquarium sank out of sight. I rested in a dead man's float but felt my mind growing fuzzy. The end was near, or so I thought.

Then the water suddenly gave way beneath me. I shrieked. I was in freefall, in a long miraculous tube of air in the middle of the ocean. I tried to grasp something, but the water walls, of course, gave no purchase. I took a deep breath, and, as I was still falling, I resumed screaming for lack of anything more productive to do.

Time to go to work. I'll send this off for now and continue later when I can.

Steve

From: bcho@seti.org
To: shanover@fnal.gov
Cc: irfan.bashir@noaa.gov

Subject: Re: My Trip

Seriously? You end your message there? Why don't you answer your phone? You are one cruel bastard, Steven Hanover.

Ben

From: shanover@fnal.gov
To: bcho@seti.org, irfan.bashir@noaa.gov
Subject: Re: My Trip

Okay, okay, don't get your panties in a bunch, Ben. I've unplugged my phone, if you must know. Anyway, I've got some time before bed. Where was I? I was falling. I was screaming.

After a few seconds it was utterly dark, and after a few more seconds the tube bent and I found myself on my back sliding on a hard, smooth surface, wet but not just water. The tube continued to bend and I gradually slowed down until I came to a stop. I lay there in shock, not prepared to begin taking stock of my situation. When my eyes had adjusted, I realized that I could identify a shape to my surroundings. There was light. I sat up and identified the source at the end of the tunnel, which was about two meters wide. I rose shakily and headed for the light.

The tunnel opened out into a great spherical room, probably 10 meters in diameter. There was a series of lights around the edge, and halfway up the wall a large platform jutted out. I noticed a ladder built into the side of the wall that led to the platform.

As I was climbing, a voice echoed in the sphere. "Dr. Hanover?" it said. I stopped climbing and listened. "Dr. Hanover, are you there?" The voice was free of affect, as if computerized. I tried to reply, but no sound came out, a result of hours on the ocean and the life-rending scream I had let out on my way down. I resumed climbing and stepped up onto the platform.

There I found a large, comfortable-looking armchair, and, on the floor next to it, a gallon jug of drinking water. Had I not been so dehydrated I think that I would have cried with joy. I staggered in gratitude to the armchair, sat down and drank and drank.

There was a monitor on the wall in front of the armchair, with a wire going to a computer on the floor. Also attached to the wall and trailing their own wires were a speaker, a microphone, and a small camera. Basic off-the-shelf equipment. The monitor displayed a familiar sight that I had not seen in 20 years or so: a fish tank screensaver, with pixelated fish, jellies and seahorses moving mechanically from side to side. I lowered the jug and let out a long belch.

"Welcome, Dr. Hanover," said the voice.

I cleared my throat as best I could and said "Hello." I sounded like a goose with a bad cold.

"Thank you for coming."

I started to protest, but then the significance of the moment finally dawned on me. Indeed, they had invited me, in their way, to this meeting, and I had accepted, had been beyond eager to come. A near death experience seemed like a steep entrance fee, but perhaps they were doing their best, and had acted in good faith. The armchair, in any case, was a nice touch. It is not every day, after all, etc...

So finally I just said, "Thank you for having me. Who's this?"

"This is Susy's Friend." He was speaking through an interpreter and a voice synthesizer. He said he was turning on his camera, and the screen flickered and went dark, though there was a shadowy blob in the middle. He asked if I could see him. When I told him it was blurry he fiddled some more. "I'm not technical," he said. The blob clarified, and another source of light flashed on from the left.

A creature floated on the screen. Kind of like a shrimp, I suppose, but I don't think it had an exoskeleton. A segmented torso, dolphin-like tail, protruding black eyes, antennae, and anywhere from eight to twelve arms. It was hard to count because they were in constant motion. It rode something like a motor-scooter without wheels, unless that was part of its body. Hard to tell.

So, he told me how when I expressed an interest in learning from them and helping them, they didn't believe me. That is, they believed that I, personally, was sincere, but that cooperation with us would not, ultimately, be to their benefit. Which, you know, I can understand.

"Our experiences with humans have been mixed," he said. "Some are nice, but others... We thought it best to maintain our distance."

But then he said that they had been very impressed with me. They felt that I had been a true friend to Suzy, and a friend of Suzy's was a friend of theirs. So they had arranged for me to meet and speak with a representative of the intelligent cephalopods!!

Look at the time! Will continue tomorrow. Good night.

Steve

From: irfan.bashir@noaa.gov
To: shanover@fnal.gov
Cc: bcho@seti.org

Subject: Re: My Trip

Sweet dreams, Steve. I have hired a man named Guido to smother you in your sleep, which is better than you deserve.

No shit? You got to talk to the smart cephalopods? Details!

Irfan

From: shanover@fnal.gov
To: bcho@seti.org, irfan.bashir@noaa.gov
Subject: Re: My Trip

Guido sends his regards.

No more cliffhangers. I promise.

So, the monitor on the wall flickered again, and a ghostly image appeared. It looked a bit like a partially collapsed umbrella, with a webbed structure at the top and a long, curved tentacle trailing down. It also had two fin-like appendages that undulated back and forth. It looked, in fact, similar to photographs of deep-sea squid that I had seen before.

The synthesized voice, which had sounded male before, said "Hello" in a higher register.

I said "Hello" back, and then there was a long, awkward pause. I panicked a little, realizing that here was my chance to ask questions of an intelligent being unknown to science, and I couldn't think of a thing to say. I was still foggy-headed from my ordeal on the ocean, and I made a flailing effort to master my faculties.

But then the voice said something interesting. She said that they, i.e. her race of intelligent cephalopods, had come into contact with humans before. At least twice that she knew of, human exploration vessels had been seen near their major population areas, but the vessels had passed by without stopping or, apparently, noticing. "I think it is because we are small," she said.

I was confused. I had imagined the creature on the monitor to be quite large, a behemoth whose great significance was matched by great physical size. But there was something out of focus moving in the background on the monitor. I realized it was one of the alien hands manipulating a control on its scooter. The cephalopod was no bigger than one of its fingers.

The male synthesized voice cut in to say, "If it helps, my little friend here is about three centimeters in length."

Maybe it was the tension of the moment, or the exhaustion, or the image of the little umbrella-shaped squid on the monitor, or the phrase "my little friend" spoken by a computer, or the realization of my own absurd assumptions, but I started laughing. I knew it was exactly the wrong thing to do, knew that it could very well go down as one of the great political blunders in history, but I couldn't help myself.

Then through the speaker: "Ha ha ha ha ha ha." Male and female synthesized voices laughing along with me.

We had a really good conversation after that. I asked Julia (the name I settled on for the squid) about how they lived, where they lived, what we could do to help them, etc. She had some questions too, though she was obviously more informed about us than I was about them. I left a thousand questions unasked, but there will be time, I hope.

When we had talked for two or three hours, I confessed that I was so tired and hungry that I didn't think I could continue. The Vogon (I told him that's what we called him, and he found that very funny) offered to take me to shore. I went back down the tunnel a ways, where there was a portal in the floor. I entered a tiny remote-controlled submarine furnished only with a rough blanket and no lighting. It was not comfortable, but the trip to San Diego took only 10 minutes.

They had a private dock where they let me out, and they spoke to me through an intercom on the outside of the submarine. After giving me directions to a nearby hotel and restaurant, they had an additional proposal for me. They were preparing an exploration deep into human territory and they wondered if I wouldn't mind going along. I would get a chance to learn more about them and how they operate, and they would get my insider's perspective on human society. The catch was that they were leaving within the hour.

Well, I told them I would go. How could I not? I went to the hotel and ate a breakfast that would choke a horse, then I went to meet the Vogons. They had a remarkable rig for their expedition: an ordinary-looking 18-wheeler ("Speedy Trucking" printed on the side) containing a huge tank for the Vogons and their equipment. I sat in the cab with an astoundingly lifelike animatronic driver, through whom they spoke to me. They told me their first stop was Las Vegas and that I should take the opportunity to sleep. I asked them how I could possibly sleep, but within a few minutes I was snoring away.

There's more to that story too, of course. Hell, next time Irfan's in town I'll allow you to get me drunk, and I promise I'll tell you anything you want to know.

Steve

From: irfan.bashir@noaa.gov
To: shanover@fnal.gov
Cc: bcho@seti.org

Subject: Re: My Trip

Arrangements made. See you this weekend.

Irfan

From: suzyeightlegs@gmail.com
To: shanover@fnal.gov
Subject: Greetings Again

Hello, Steve! I hope you are doing well. I am fine, but I have been feeling a little bit homesick. Remember my little aquarium? It was so long ago that I lived there, and you gave me puzzles to solve. But it wasn't really that long ago, was it?

I was very scared when I lost you in the water, and the water was so deep, and I didn't know where to go. But they helped me, and now I have a nice little cave, and there are clams and crabs to eat. I like it here.

They were right about the ocean. It is interesting and there are lots of good things to eat. But also I was right about the ocean, because it is scary sometimes.

I understand now what it means that life is cruel.

From: shanover@fnal.gov
To: suzyeightlegs@gmail.com
Subject: Re: Greetings Again

Dear Suzy,

It's good to hear from you again, my friend. My office is quite dull without you. I miss you, but I'm glad that you are settling into your new home.

I have not had much first-hand experience with the cruelty of life, having lived my life in a sort of aquarium myself. Please take care of yourself down there, Suzy, and let me know how you are getting along. I may have a new email address soon. I will let you know.

Steve

From: shanover@fnal.gov
To: staff@fnal.gov
Subject: Moving OnDear Friends and Colleagues,

As most of you know, Friday will be my last day at Fermilab. I will cherish my years here. I have never for a moment wavered in my support for the work that

Fermilab does, nor in my admiration for the awesomely talented and dedicated people that do it.

I will be honest. I have gotten a lot of strange looks and pointed questions lately. If I were leaving to "spend more time with my family," it probably would have been easier for people to accept. That I am leaving to become a lowly truck driver does not compute. So I thought it would be good to take a moment to explain myself.

I will spare you the childhood story of seeing a truck driver at a highway rest stop, his gruff amiability, the magnificent rumbling, gleaming beast he stepped into, the wink he gave me before setting his sight on the road ahead and pulling away. That happened, but it's not why I'm taking the job with Speedy Trucking.

Speedy Trucking is employee-owned and offers an unusual amount of autonomy to its drivers. My schedule will be flexible and will afford me plenty of time to engage in my favorite hobbies (astronomy, scuba diving) as well as, incidentally, spend more time with my family (assuming they will have me).

Also, I have always been attracted to life on the road, the opportunities for discovery in the small, overlooked spaces of life. At Fermilab, we work on the big questions. I am looking forward to spending some time working on some of the smaller ones.

This explanation will likely be unsatisfactory to many of you, to which I can only wink, set my eyes on the road, and be on my way.

Best Regards,

Steve

From: irfan.bashir@noaa.gov
To: bcho@seti.org
Subject: Re: Steve

You should have seen him, Ben. Like a fish. I couldn't keep up with him.

He took me down to Suzy's cave, and he knocked on this rock all casual. Your average social visit. When the octopus came out they swam around each other like it was olympic water ballet. They scooted off and later I learned they went to look at a particular patch of pretty coral that Suzy had found.

I assume you know he moved to San Diego? He doesn't drive the truck that much, maybe 3 weeks out of the year. He showed me his workshop where he's made a prototype for a new thermostat that automatically adjusts to the preferences of the animal. It works with octopuses and squid so far. He says it will be cheap and super-reliable. He talks like a kid hopped up on frosted flakes. "It's going to revolutionize the industry!" he says. Also he wants to market the traveling aquariums and has about a million applications for the artificial water the Vogons developed.

He's doing some other stuff too that he didn't want to talk about. He had some kind of building schematic on his desk that he turned over so I couldn't see it. He actually put his finger on the side of his nose and winked at me. I'm just like, whatever dude. He's got his big-thumbed shrimp buddies now, I guess.

Irfan

From: steve@speedytrucking.com
To: gruntbuggly@speedytrucking.com
Subject: Delivery Status Notification

Your package is en route and is scheduled to be delivered tomorrow by 8pm.

The occupant of said package is an *Enteroctopus dofleini* named Stanley. He is nervous and stressed but otherwise unharmed. He will be hungry on arrival!

Stanley's former caretakers will be very surprised in the morning to find that their last-minute security precautions proved totally inadequate. If only they had spent half as much time providing for the needs of their prisoner!

I am tired but exhilarated and looking forward to our trip next week. I'm deeply honored to be allowed to tag along on an extraterrestrial mission, and pleased that Suzy will be there too. I'm a bit scared, to be honest, to face the immensity of space, but comforted to know that I will be among friends.

Steve

About the story

My family and I were staying in a small cabin in Shenandoah National Park. After dinner, despite having hiked most of the afternoon, and despite the fog, I decided I would go on my usual after-dinner walk and listen to my usual podcasts, damn it. I began walking south along the Appalachian Trail and listening to *This American Life*.

In this particular episode of *This American Life*, someone was talking about how Fermi's Paradox — the idea that if the universe abounds with intelligent life, we should have heard from it by now — made him sad. I.e. it made him sad to think that we are alone in the universe. I listened to this as the fog grew denser along the trail, and I felt annoyed. What about all of the life on Earth that we barely understood? What about the 95% of the ocean that remained completely unexplored? I knew it was silly feeling annoyed at someone feeling sad, as I trusted vaguely in the fact that the Appalachian Trail was very well-marked and there was little chance of me getting off the path despite the fog. But really, to say that the lack of extraterrestrial intelligence millions of light-years away (if indeed there were none) meant that we were "alone," despite the truly glorious variety of strange and interesting creatures here on Earth, bothered me. Vine-covered tree trunks moved in and out of the mist, sunset giving everything a yellowish hue, and I felt the thrill of the realization that I had, perhaps, by this time, gone as far away from our little cabin as I could safely go that evening. I turned around, and as I reeled in the trail I thought about whether and how I could turn my unreasonable annoyance into a story. Something funny, preferably.

A question for the author

Q: Do you use critique groups or other resources to polish your writing?

A: My critique group consists of my wife and my mother, who are both writers. They offer invaluable feedback, but I realize that it may not always be impartial or thorough. I have a Scribophile account, and I think it would be a very useful resource if I could manage to use it more often. I go back to Scribophile every once in a while to give it another try, and when I do I generally manage to do one critique, and then when I try to do another one I slip into a state of paralysis and self-doubt. Who am I to analyze this story? Am I being too harsh, too picky, too glib, too nice? I don't manage to finish the second critique, because I run out of time, and I rationalize my behavior by reasoning that I am better off using my time reading the books on my Goodreads list and writing my own stories than critiquing the stories of others. This is true to some extent, but it's also selfish and maybe self-defeating in the long run.

About the author

David Hammond lives and dreams in Virginia with his wife and two daughters. During the day, he makes websites. More of his writing can be found at oldshoepress.com.

Chasing the Light

Gloria Wickman

Markus stood on the rocky hill in front of his house, neck aching as he craned it toward the sky. He'd been waiting for hours. He'd snuck early out of bed, slinking his way through the house and slipping outside into the muggy morning air. He'd climbed the hill, using his hands to steady himself as the ground slipped and slid beneath him, until he reached the highest point in the village. When the light came, he'd be the first to see it.

It came only once a year, the light, the bringer of the harvest. Markus squinted his eyes and his chest jumped as he saw it. A pinprick of light, duller than even the stars. It grew slowly, flickering and pulsating dimly like blood pumping from a heart.

Markus hopped from foot to foot, shaking his hands out as he waited for *the moment.*

The light grew brighter, then exploded out in every direction as it descended onto the land below. It rushed over the empty fields in a wave, inundating them with a warm, bright yellow glow. The dirt, plowed neatly into hills and furrows, shook and came alive as tiny, wispy white tendrils peeked out of the earth and opened their first leaves to the light.

The light surrounded Markus, covering his skin and hair in a cool and tingling mass of tiny bodies, like animate grains of sand glowing and shimmering as they darted around his face. Individually, their movement was erratic, drifting and surging one direction to another even as the swarm itself flew ever forward. But together there was a sense of harmony, no collisions between pieces of the light, each one shifting slightly to accommodate the others. A kind of peaceful chaos.

Markus blinked, fighting to look but unable to keep his eyes open, like trying to see in a rainstorm. Then it was gone.

The light never lingered long. It whooshed past him and the village and down into the valley.

Markus ran. He chased after the light with a child's spirit, never doubting he would catch it, even as it faded further and further in the distance. He ran until the last of the light disappeared over the horizon and he doubled over trying to catch his breath. Sweat glistened on his forehead and trickled down the back of his neck.

He laughed. Next year he'd catch it for sure. He turned back toward the village and the sound of his neighbors singing and shouting grew softly as he returned. His mother and father passed mugs of lager to each other, toasting to the light as their crops lived a lifecycle in a day, first blossoming, then turning heavy with fruit and grain.

Markus reached for his own glass and joined the dancing and revelry the light had left in its wake.

One day the light stopped coming.

Markus had grown old, too old to chase after the light, but not too old to sit out in his rocking chair and stare up at the sky.

At first, Markus thought it was his eyesight going. He'd lost track of some of the old stars; it was natural he might not see the light when it was still far out. But as time crept on, uneasiness settled in his stomach and crawled up the back of his throat. Voices murmured around him in hushed tones. Parents snapped at their children to hush and quit playing.

"Maybe it's just a little late this year. Took a wrong turn at the last rock," someone said.

A few uneasy laughs answered him. The hours drew on, and one by one the people left to go back into their homes. A few were sobbing, but most just moved numbly, their necks bent toward the sky, looking for anything, any sign of hope.

Markus stayed on his porch, waiting, watching. The village slept and awoke in the same darkness that hung overhead every day the light didn't come.

The first day was for blaming. The hushed, fearful whispers turned to shouted accusations. It was the flyers that did it. They stole the light, or killed it, or did something to scare it off. People stared up at the darting specks of light in the sky, the stars that moved this way and that in an angular, incomprehensible dance—*the flyers*—and cursed their names.

One woman, words slurred with despair and drunkenness, picked up a stone and threw it toward the sky. More rocks followed. Everyone seemed to carry one in their hand. They yelled and whooped and made promises about what would happen to any flyer unlucky enough crash near them.

Markus sat on his porch, looking up at the sky.

The second day was for planning. Anger gave way to fatigue and discussions on how to survive a year without a harvest. There were some food stores. Baskets and barrels of grains and dried fruit sat in the cellars of every home, and even more was kept in the town center. Hunger would come slowly, growing and spreading like a crop of its own.

Markus worked while the village slept, loading up his handcart with all his stores from the previous harvest. He'd lived frugally, and much remained. He loaded several heavy baskets of grain and boxes of the sweet dried fruit that stained his teeth even after many weeks of being preserved. Carefully, he nestled a round terra cotta jar between two grain baskets. The jar was stuffed with nuts his niece had gifted him from her resurrection tree, the only plant that stayed alive between visits of the light, slipping into dormancy until it was reawakened by those tiny, dancing organisms.

Markus walked slowly out of town, not returning until the first of his neighbors had crept out of their homes. He waved as he returned emptyhanded to his front porch. No one asked where he had gone.

The twenty-ninth day was for math. Markus heard it through whispers. Half a year of food for two people is a year of food for one. An old man, perhaps too old to even to live to the next harvest, would be better off if he died sooner, left his resources to the younger and more able bodied.

Markus left the town on the thirtieth day. He passed by the fields, ruined by neglect and fits of rage, the neat furrows pushed over and smashed into lumps of soil and broken ale bottles. He kept walking until his house, the house he'd long pictured staying in until he passed

from the world, disappeared on the
horizon.

Markus had found the cave when he was
a boy. The light had showed it to him,
back when he had the legs to chase after
it. He had followed the light over a ridge,
stumbled, and fallen into a deep pit.
Quick reflexes and a love of tumbling
saved him from broken bones, but he had
cut his hands and knees on the ground
and hissed at their stinging. He looked
above him, too high above him, at the hole
and the sky desperately out of reach.

He had panicked. He felt around the
walls of the too large cavern, trying to find
a place to climb up and out. He'd jumped,
and screamed, and tried to scamper up
the walls, but he only rubbed more dirt
and rock into his cuts and made his voice
go hoarse and scratchy.

Hours later, he sat down at the bottom
of the pit and cried. He kept his eyes on
the ground, unable to look at the place
above him he wanted so desperately to be.
Then, in that total blackness, he saw a
light. One single piece of the light that
must have fallen in with him.

He stared at it as it danced around him and reached a hand out to touch it. It skittered away, and Markus felt a sudden sickness seize him, the realization that it could go where he couldn't, that sooner or later it would fly up and away and leave him behind. But the light kept dancing, floating in front of him and around him, lazily swooping side to side.

Markus watched the light flitter through the cavern, riding tiny air currents he couldn't feel. Then, impossibly, it glided against one of the walls and disappeared. Markus jumped to his feet and rushed to wear he'd last seen it.

He found a small gap, a gap not much wider than his body, which led to a narrow tunnel. Markus raced down it, bumping against the stone walls until he reached a short shaft. He looked up and saw the sky.

High above Markus, the flyers darted in front of the long, hazy clouds that astronomers said was an arm of the galaxy, stretching out with a million worlds just like his.

Markus watched the flyers as he climbed up the narrow shaft, squeezing his fingers into the jagged rock and stretching his toes out to balance. They said the flyers traveled between many strange worlds. Worlds full of air that couldn't be breathed. Worlds where the light was so bright it blocked out the stars for hours at a time and painted the sky blue.

Markus pulled himself onto the surface and flipped onto his back, breathing deeply with relief as he looked up at the sky. Staring at the hazy clouds, he tried to imagine what those other worlds would be like. A bright blue sky, and colors everywhere on the ground, as bright as when the light came. It sounded wondrous. It sounded frightening, too much good overloading the senses, the stomachache after a feast.

Markus squeezed his eyes shut for a moment to picture it, then he exhaled and got to his feet, preparing himself for the long walk home. He never told anyone about what happened that day. Instead, he'd bitten his lip, and sat quietly at the dinner table, smiling when he thought no one was looking. The cave became his secret place, a shelter when he needed to get away.

The trail of fire burned across the sky brighter than anything Markus had seen in two planetary revolutions. The sound, a deep rumbling wave accompanied by the hissing of sizzling metal, crashed against his chest a few moments later. The trail ended in a puff of smoke and a bang that was jarringly late, as though the world had fallen out of sync.

A flyer.

Markus chased after it. His shoes, now no more than thick wrapped bundles of cloth, sank into the ashy ground as he trudged on. His path took him near the town, but he heard no sounds as he approached, no laughter, no tears. During the long absence of the light, his world had died. It wasn't rotten so much as mummified.

Smoke billowed in the distance, inky black against the dark gray horizon. Monotone colors as desiccated as the landscape.

Markus kept moving. Past the crumbled sandstone buildings, past the bent and twisted metal poking out of the ground like withered stalks, past his own house, as ruined as the rest, the ceiling collapsed inward, the porch scorched black from an explosion, the few belongings he'd left behind stolen or scattered around the broken doorway. His chair had lost a leg, but still sat stubbornly upright, leaning against the wall to stare at the stars.

Markus didn't stop until he reached the flyer.

The flames burned themselves out before Markus arrived. Still, he felt their heat as he approached, a dryness in air that always felt heavy and wet, and he tasted smoke flavored with metal and acid. The wreck, a grotesque corpse of broken and twisted metal, had wings like a bird, and a long, slender body. Markus circled the wreck slowly, studying it.

A single set of footprints, uneven, and drawn out in long divots by dragging feet, led away from the flyer toward the rocky hills along the horizon. A drop of moisture, not water and not oil, darkened the ashy gray dust around the prints.

He'd seen enough blood in the last year to develop a sense for it. The first few times it had come with a rush of fear and adrenaline, a tickle at the back of his throat, a sudden anxiousness and need to flee. Now it only made him wary, more careful and conscious of his next move.

He needed to find the pilot. Others would be around soon.

Markus followed the tracks toward the hills. The pilot had fallen once on their way up the incline, leaving a smeared set of palm prints in the sand and another bit of blood on the rocks. Their hands looked small, smaller than the booted footprints would have suggested.

As Markus crested over the first hill, stepping carefully on the sand and rocks that threatened to pour down with each step, he saw the pilot resting on the ground halfway down into the next valley. She kept one hand pressed firmly against her stomach and breathed heavily.

Her clothes were strange. But then, what must he look like to her? An old man with a beard that hung around his face like wispy white clouds, fabric torn and mended and torn again hanging too loosely from his thinning body. He ran a hand over his hair and beard, trying to tame them a bit before he stepped closer.

The pilot jolted back when Markus moved forward. One hand flew toward her jacket to reach something, but couldn't find it. She hissed as the movement pulled against her wound, but then clamped her jaw shut in a thin, firm line.

"Who the hell are you?" The pilot hissed as she struggled to her feet, eyes never leaving Markus.

"My name is Markus," he said, offering a soft smile. "Did you fall from the sky?"

The pilot started to shake her head, and her face contorted into a frown as she looked for a lie. Finding none, she shrugged. "I guess you could say that."

"Are you hurt?"

"I'll live."

Markus bit his lip, uncertain what to say next. "I have medical supplies. And food. Not far from here."

The pilot studied Markus carefully, eyes moving quickly from his wizened face to his tall but lanky frame. Though he pretended not to notice, Markus could see the calculation in her face, wondering if she could trust him, wondering if she could fight him off if she were wrong.

"Okay," the pilot sighed as she stepped toward him. She kept her right hand pressed against her side. Blood oozed slowly between her fingers.

The pilot never complained about the distance they walked, though it must have pained her. She followed a step behind Markus and her head swiveled from him to the rocky crags and torn up fields surrounding them.

The pilot sniffed once and Markus looked behind him to see that she was holding back tears. Markus wondered how old she was, though he knew she had to be not much past twenty years. Her skin was a shade lighter than his, though still a deep, rich brown, and aside from a scar on her left cheek, she had none of the marks time had left on Markus's face.

Their eyes met for a moment, but the pilot's gaze warned him not to ask about her. Markus nodded and continued walking.

"We're here," Markus said, after a long passage of silence. He stopped in front of a large boulder shaped like a man squatting down. The rock, porous and volcanic, was lighter than it appeared, like a dried husk of a rock slowly rolling across the landscape.

Markus bent down and his spine popped softly. The pilot's eyes shifted to him at the sound. "Just my old bones," he said as he brushed a thin layer of dirt off the ground and revealed a misshapen trap door constructed of the same dull-gray metal as the destroyed flyer.

Markus yanked on the door's handle and it groaned open.

"You go down first," Markus said.

The pilot glanced uncertainly at the hole. There was a ladder, a rickety frame made of tree branches roped together, attached to a stone wall. The bottom of the pit was invisible, melting into a cloud of black about five rungs down.

The pilot glanced at Markus once more. Then she shrugged and grabbed hold of the ladder, quickly sliding into the darkness below.

Markus moved more slowly, taking three steps down before reaching back to grab the trapdoor and pulling it over his head. Without even starlight to guide him, Markus stepped down the ladder, not needing to see to know where he was.

"It's dark down here," the pilot said quietly as Markus's feet thudded against the dirt at the base of the ladder.

Markus took a couple of steps into the room and pulled his lantern from a metal crate he kept near the ladder. His hands and feet moved automatically, well-practiced with moving in the dark. A small orb of light illuminated the room as he switched it on and Markus saw the pilot standing with her hands out in front of her, ready for an attack as she kept her back pressed against the wall.

"Bit of a loose wire, I think," Markus said as he tapped the metal casing of the lantern.

The pilot stepped away from the wall and glanced around. The light only dimly reached the farthest walls, the whole space being no more than twelve paces long and perhaps eight wide. The light reflected softly off a table near the center of the room.

"Thank you. For helping me," the pilot said.

Markus nodded.

"My name's Angie," she added, shoulders slumping a bit as she lowered herself to sit on the floor.

"Angie? I had a niece with that name," Marcus said as he opened a trunk in the corner of the room and started to dig through it. "She passed on, well, sooner than she should've." He stood and walked over to Angie a moment later, passing her a roll of bandages and a tin bottle of water.

"I'm sorry."

Angie took the supplies and poured some of the water on her side, hissing as the liquid made contact with her skin. She pressed the bandages against her wound, a cut that looked much shallower now that the blood had been cleared away.

"This salve should help," Markus said as he handed her a mostly empty jar of an ash colored cream. "It's saved my life a few times."

"What's it like up there?" Markus asked, unable to hold the question back any longer. He slurped another spoonful of porridge into his mouth. The mixture was tasteless and soupy. He'd started adding more water to it, hoping to stretch his provisions a bit further.

Angie had stayed with him over a week. Her side was healing and uninfected and she'd grown restless, offering to repay Markus by cleaning and scavenging. Markus gave her tasks, little things that didn't really need doing, but she did each of them with vigor.

"What's it like up there?" Angie tilted her head as she repeated the question. "Bright. I never thought about it really, but it's bright." She swallowed. "You know I'd never been to a planet before? I used to dream about what it'd be like, to have so much freedom. To be able to go anywhere without walls and air tanks and pressure suits."

Markus hummed. "I always wanted to fly. Be part of the dancing lights in the sky."

Angie laughed and her spoon clanked against the edge of her dish. "We don't dance, I'm afraid. It's mostly just mining and hauling big space rocks to the nearest processing system."

"It still looks beautiful."

"Only from a distance." Angie sighed. "But it was home."

Markus dropped the spoon back into his empty bowl and looked thoughtfully at Angie. "There's something I want to show you."

Picking up the lantern from the table, Markus led Angie down a narrow tunnel at the back of the room. He heard a soft rustling behind him as the jagged stone edges of the wall scraped lightly against Angie's skin and stalactites tugged at her hair. The tunnel curved to the right, then expanded into a large, open cavern.

"It's not finished yet, but with your help it could be," Markus said, walking toward the center of the cavern.

A flyer. Nestled in the cave like a fox in a burrow, sheltered from the elements and the people that would tear it to pieces as a proxy for their anguish. Even in the dim light of Markus's lantern, the flyer was a patchwork beast, stitched and riveted together from the dead ships that had fallen before it.

Angie darted toward the flyer, running her hand along the metal wing, fingers catching in the pits and gouges that peppered its body. She reached up, grabbing the rim of the cockpit, and hoisted herself inside with a jump.

Angie slid easily behind the controls. Her hands glided over the switches and gauges and then back to the control stick. She pushed on it experimentally, feeling the familiar pressure of it tugging back at her.

"Not bad, old man," she said. Then her brow furrowed. "But how did you get it here?"

Markus laughed. "I flew it. Kind of. Mostly." He coughed.

"Mostly?" Angie asked.

"I found a wreck on the other side of ridge, about half a day's walk from where you crashed. It had been sitting there awhile before I got there, dust covering everything."

"No pilot?"

Markus rubbed his mouth. "He was already dead—murdered—when I got there. My people," Markus sighed. "My people don't act much like people anymore. Anyway, some of the metal had been scavenged off it, along with the seat and anything else people thought they could use, but the frame was intact and the engine seemed more or less alright, so I figured, what the hell, let's see what this thing can do, right?"

"That's pretty dangerous."

"I know. It was stupid, really. But I didn't care back then. The light was gone. My niece was gone. And I figured the worst that could happen was dying. And that didn't seem like much of a bad thing at the time," Markus said quietly. "So I climbed in, fired it up, and promptly got knocked on my behind as it started skimming over the ground, black smoke coming up everywhere behind me. I figured that stick thing directed it around, and I managed to more or less guide it back this way."

"I'm impressed you managed to land it down here," Angie said.

Markus chuckled and rubbed the back of his neck. "I actually tried to land it on the ridge above us but I slid and kind of tumbled in here." He glanced at the hole in the rock above them. "Bit of a pattern for me, really," he added. "It took me days to get it upright again, and I had to take most of it apart and put it back together. It got me thinking that it wasn't all that complicated after all. There was a chance I could get it working again. I've gone to a few other wrecks and scavenged smaller pieces off of them, and repurposed some of my stuff for it, but I could use another pair of hands. And a pilot to teach me to fly it properly."

Angie smiled. "I might be able to help with that."

"What happened to this place?" Angie asked. She lay underneath the flyer, hands caked with grease and soot as she dug through a mess of wires. She hissed as two of them touched and sparked against each other.

"Same thing that happened everywhere," Markus said. He sat under the left wing, fiddling with a blackened mass of burnt wiring and half-melted metal. "The light stopped coming and it died. Things turned ugly. Those of us that are left avoid each other when we can, fight when we can't."

Angie peeked her head out from under the flyer. "What do you mean the light stopped coming?"

"The light. *The light,*" Markus's eyes widened and the metal fell forgotten beside him. "You really don't know?"

Angie shook her head.

"It comes from, I don't know, up there somewhere," Markus gestured above his head. "Some kind of swarm from space, like tiny little bugs is what people used to say. They'd swoop out of the sky like a miracle each year and everything would start to grow. Flowers, fruits, grains, everything. Then one day they stopped coming. People gave up hope. Then they gave up on each other."

Markus sighed. "We had some food stored, of course, and there are a lot less of us running around than there used to be," Markus turned his head away. "But I'd guess we've probably got less than a year before the end of everything."

Angie bit her lip. "And that's why you rebuilt the flyer, why you rescued me. You want to take shelter in the sky."

Markus shook his head, standing up from under the wing. "No. No, I'm going to bring the light back. It's just gotten a little lost. I'm going to bring it back home."

Angie pulled herself out from underneath the flyer, wiping her hand on a dirty cloth before tossing it back on the ground. "So you know where this light of yours is?"

"No," Markus said.

"You know how to bring it back once you find it?"

"No idea."

Angie sighed. "So it's just wishful thinking, then. False hope."

Markus gently tapped his hand against the wing of the flyer. "I wouldn't say that. Sometimes you have to run after the things you don't know you can catch. That's the only way to move forward. Besides, I have you to help me now."

Angie bit her lip and grabbed another wrench.

Markus awoke slowly, shaken to consciousness by a low rumble that tumbled through the tunnels and echoed off the walls even as it faded into nothingness. It was only after the reverberations stilled and silence stuffed his ears like cotton that he jolted upright.

The flyer. Markus scrambled down the tunnel, feet slipping on the dirt and the narrow walls tearing at his clothes as he hurried to confirm what he already knew. Angie was gone. So was the flyer.

Markus saw a grease stain where the flyer had stood, one more black mark in a place already eaten by darkness. Markus slid to his knees. Hours passed. The light from his lantern faded and died.

The sky stayed dark. Sometimes Markus sat on the surface and watched the flyers dance in the sky. He wondered if any of them were Angie. He wondered if she ever looked back down on the surface to see him looking up at her.

When Markus was a boy, the light had seemed brighter than anything he had seen. He remembered watching it roll over the hills, coating the fields with a golden glow and sticking to every building like a glittery film.

In those days, there were colors. Greens and blues and reds and deep rich browns. It was so beautiful that he never minded that it came just once a year.

This light looked different than he remembered, though Markus couldn't say in what way. Maybe it was a bit older, a bit sicker, maybe it was tired from traveling all that way across the stars.

Markus had never seen anything more beautiful.

Markus glimpsed high overhead, drifting and growing bigger as it undulated toward him.

Markus put a hand to his mouth, choked on a sob as he watched the light move closer. Unhurried, waving and swooping to the sides and even retreating on itself before surging forward again.

Markus watched it for minutes before he heard it. He'd forgotten it had a sound, a low hum that he felt with his chest more than his ears.

The light came closer and Markus saw the first bits of color blossom on the ground.

Greens. The greens were always first. They wiggled and hopped out of the ground dancing to the hum of the light. The flowers would come next. Blues and yellows and violets blooming into red fruits.

A chorus, a hundred voices shouting and crying and laughing, welled up over the rocky hills and shifting earth. Markus's throat tickled and he realized his own voice was calling out among them, sounding out the same relief and euphoria together with everyone.

Together.

Markus hadn't felt together for a long time.

Markus heard the thrum of the flyer's engine before he saw it, a tiny splotch of black in front of the sea of light. The flyer passed overhead, and Markus saw it dragging a large rock behind it, the light melting off of the rock in waves. In the next second, the light hit him, almost blinding him as it flew past. A million billion dancers paraded around him, bringing the dead land back to life. He stood immobile, letting the light touch him and watching it flicker past.

As the last of the light flew past him, Markus turned and started to run, chasing the light until it disappeared over the horizon.

About the story

I wrote "Chasing the Light," somewhat differently from my typical process. Usually I tend to heavily outline and focus on plot and characters before anything else. But this time I focused much more on the emotional beats and tone of the story and then the plot developed from those feelings.

There were two main sources of inspiration for the story. The first was an image in my head of the light coming down onto a dark and dead field and reviving it. This became the foundation of the final scene of the story, though the addition of the people cheering and shouting in relief is also a reflection of what I witnessed during the total solar eclipse in my hometown last August. It was a truly unique experience to stand outside in my backyard and just hear everyone in the city cheering together for the same event. It was a moment unlike anything else I've experienced and came with a profound sense of community and shared human experience.

The second source of inspiration was a line from the song "Sea" by BTS. "Where there is hope, there are trials." The ending of the story needed to have feelings of both relief and euphoria, but I wanted the scenes before that to examine hope and how it exists alongside darkness and despair.

There's an old cliché that it's always darkest before the dawn, but for me this story is about the hope that another dawn will come. Markus does his best to help bring it, both by constructing a new flyer and by caring for the people around him. However, the final outcome is out of his hands by a certain measure, because hope exists alongside powerlessness.

A question for the author

Q: Do you often include children in your stories? What role do they play?

A: I haven't included many children in my stories, but when I have it's usually been to illustrate an episode early in a character's life. I don't think of writing children any differently than any other characters, so they could play any role depending on the context of the story.

What's most important to me when writing is that every character, even minor ones, has a sense of agency in their actions so I'm always wary of stories that treat children more like talking props or symbols of innocence rather than fleshed out individuals.

About the author

Gloria Wickman is a speculative fiction and comics writer currently residing in Wyoming. She has a B.A. in anthropology and has always been fascinated with the roles language and culture serve in behavior. When she's not writing, she's usually studying Korean or spending time at the park.

gloriawickman.com

Copyright

Metaphorosis Publishing

Metaphorosis offers beautifully written science fiction and fantasy. Our projects include:

Metaphorosis Magazine

Metaphorosis, a weekly magazine of SFF short stories, including stories from all the authors in this anthology. Find out more at magazine.metaphorosis.com, and sign up to be notified of new stories.

Metaphorosis Books

Recent books from Metaphorosis can be found at <u>books.metaphorosis.com</u>, and include:

Metaphorosis 2017

Metaphorosis 2016

All the stories from *Metaphorosis* magazine's second year.

Almost all the stories from *Metaphorosis* magazine's first year.

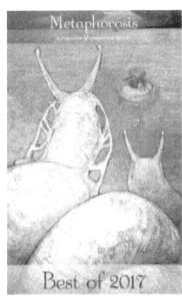

**Metaphorosis:
Best of 2017**

**Metaphorosis:
Best of 2016**

The best science
fiction and fantasy
stories from
Metaphorosis' 2nd
year.

The best science
fiction and fantasy
stories from
Metaphorosis' 1st
year.

Reading 5X5

Reading 5X5

Five stories, five times

Writers' Edition

Twenty-five SFF authors, five base stories, five versions of each – see how different writers take on the same material.

All the stories from the regular, readers' edition, plus two extra stories, the story seed, and authors' notes.

Best Vegan SFF of 2017

Best Vegan SFF of 2016

The best vegan science fiction and fantasy stories of 2017!

The best vegan science fiction and fantasy stories of 2016!

Susurrus

A darkly romantic story of magic, love, and suffering.

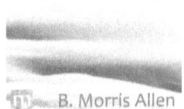